Changeling Press. LLC

ChangelingPress.com

Chase/Doc Duet
A Bones MC Romance
Marteeka Karland

Chase/Doc Duet
A Bones MC Romance
Marteeka Karland

All rights reserved.
Copyright ©2024 Marteeka Karland

ISBN: 978-1-60521-888-5

Publisher:
Changeling Press LLC
315 N. Centre St.
Martinsburg, WV 25404
ChangelingPress.com

Printed in the U.S.A.

Editor: Katriena Knights
Cover Artist: Marteeka Karland

The individual stories in this anthology have been previously released in E-Book format.

Table of Contents

Chase (Bones MC 12)
A Bones MC Romance
Marteeka Karland

Cotton: When I avenged my sister's murder, I knew the consequences. I was just fifteen when I was arrested, but I've never regretted taking the law into my own hands. Now I'm on parole and the father of the man I killed is a judge. I can't seem to catch a break. The ten years I gave the state might not be enough. Then Chase steamrolls into my life. Though he means to protect me, I know this man has the power to tear out my heart.

Chase: I've spent the better part of my life in the shadows. I can't seem to atone for the sins of my past. No matter what I do, those demons still haunt me. The moment I spot Cotton, everything changes. Everything about the girl screams "battered woman," but she's more than that. There's death in her eyes. She's killed, but she's no killer. I will protect her till my last breath. Because she's my only salvation. She's my woman.

Chapter One

Cotton

"Watch where you're fuckin' goin', bitch!"

The old guy behind the wheel of the truck that almost ran me over at a crosswalk blew his horn and shook his fist as he leaned out the window and yelled at me. I ignored him, hunching in on myself as I hurried across the street. It wasn't my fault he wanted to run the red light at the intersection. Most people did here, when there wasn't anything coming.

It was pouring down rain and even with an umbrella, I was already soaking wet from head to toe. It was why I'd put my work clothes in my backpack before heading out. I didn't have a car, and even if I had one, I didn't have a license. I'd been here three weeks and had finally managed to score a job in a biker bar. The only one in Somerset, Kentucky. The walk was longer than I liked, but it was the only place that would hire me. I was a convicted felon. And not just any felony. Murder. Well, manslaughter. And only because I'd pleaded down. The original charge had been first degree murder and I had no illusion the prosecutor would have gone for life in prison. No. If they'd managed to convict me of capital murder, my ass would have been on the wrong end of a lethal injection.

Whoever said prison time is slow time had it right. Or maybe it was just my youth. I'd been convicted of murder when I was fifteen and had spent the next ten years of my life in prison, patiently waiting for the day I got out. I'd paid my dues and then some. But never once did I regret killing the bastard who'd raped and murdered my big sister. Which was a problem at my probation hearings. It was why I'd done ten years instead of four out of the fifteen I was given. As far as I was concerned, the bastard had got what he'd deserved. Unfortunately, that man had been the son of a prominent judge. Even though my lawyer was supposed to be on my side, it was painfully obvious he wasn't. Which likely played a large part in my parole.

So I'd kept my mouth shut, done my time, then made it to this little town where I could hopefully disappear into the rustic scenery. The terms of my probation stipulated I had to stay in Kentucky. They didn't specify where. Only that I had to tell them where I was going and check in with a probation officer they assigned in the area. My sentence was originally for fifteen years, so I still had five years' probation. Perhaps working in a bar wasn't the best place to keep my nose clean, but even though most employers were more lenient than they used to be, with the violent crime I'd been convicted of, everywhere I'd applied had given me a hard pass. I honestly couldn't say I blamed them.

The Boneyard had been different. They'd only requested to know who my probation officer was so they could get a hard copy of the terms I had to follow. The people I'd met who ran the place hadn't judged me, only told me to let them know the second I felt I might be in trouble. They didn't want blowback coming to their bar if I fucked up, but they also had said they'd help any way they could. I wasn't sure I believed the last, but I'd do my best not to repay their kindness in hiring me with getting my ass arrested for a probation violation.

I hurried into the back entrance, trying my best not to drip all over the floor. It was a losing battle because I was drenched.

"Girl, what the fuck?" Pops, the grizzled biker

who ran the bar frowned at me, likely seeing the puddle as I stuffed my umbrella into a plastic grocery sack and hung it on a peg next to the door.

"I'm sorry, Pops. I'll clean it up. Just let me change clothes."

"Don't give a fuck about the water. Why are you soaked to the fuckin' skin?"

I cringed back. It was a reflex I couldn't seem to break myself from. I worked so hard in prison to avoid any kind of conflict I usually just rolled over and showed my belly, making it no fun for the bullies. It made for hard going at first, and Lord knew I took some horrible beatings, but, in the end, it had paid off. The gangs were too afraid to make me traffic their drugs or anything else because they knew I'd give up at the first sign of trouble, and I wasn't any fun to beat up because I never fought back. The only problem had been from the guards. There was no getting away from the guards.

"I'm sorry. I know I'm probably not decent. I was just going to change clothes."

He sighed. "Girl, stop. Take a breath." I know I stared wide-eyed at the older man, but I couldn't help it. The only men I'd had contact with the last ten years had been prison guards. And they never had my best interest at heart. This guy was more intimidating than anyone I'd ever met. I did as he instructed but only because I knew from experience, he'd keep me there until he got what he wanted. So I did what I was told. Just like I'd learned in prison.

"Now, tell me why you look like a drowned rat."

"Because it's raining?"

"Yeah. I can see that. Pourin'. Why the hell were you out in it?"

I blinked. "Uh, I had to get to work, Pops."

He stared at me for several moments, his gaze piercing me uncomfortably. It was like the man was trying to look into my soul and find the answers to all his questions. So far, he hadn't asked me about my time in prison or my version of the events leading up to it, but I figured it was just a matter of time. If he gave me this particular look, there was no way I'd be able to not tell him. If he asked. I wasn't volunteering anything.

"Did you walk to work, Cotton?"

"Yes, sir." I looked down at my feet, fidgeting uncomfortably.

"Why didn't you call the compound like I told you to?"

"What?" I chanced a glance up at him.

"I told you if you needed anything you were to call the compound or me and we'd make sure you were taken care of." He sounded -- and looked -- angry as fuck but he didn't raise his voice.

"Well, I didn't see a need to bother anyone. I'm perfectly capable of getting to work on my own."

"You could have called a taxi. Or, better yet, called me. I'd have sent one of the boys after you."

"What does it matter, Pops? I'm here. I'd have already changed if you hadn't stopped me. I'm not late. The bar doesn't open for another hour." I didn't mean it to sound belligerent, though the second I uttered the words, I knew I probably did. I was genuinely confused. Why would he want to help me?

"It fuckin' matters because it's fuckin' pouring the fuckin' rain, Cotton! You'll catch your death out in this shit! Besides, if you're still living in that fleabag motel, it's too far for you to be walking. You could get hurt."

"I'm fine. Really. It's not cold outside or

anything. Now, I need to change. Then I'll clean up my mess."

With a scowl, Pops muttered something about "damned stubborn girl" as he turned and stalked away from me. I ducked my head and hurried into the bathroom where I put on my (mostly) dry clothes and went back out to mop up my mess. Pops was just finishing up with the mop. He glared at me before shaking his head and turning his back on me.

"You need a keeper, girl," he said over his shoulder.

"I've been kept too long," I said softly. "I just want to make a new life for myself and be left alone. I didn't mean to be a problem, Pops. I won't be again."

Pops scowled and grunted before walking away from me. I went to the front of the bar to get ready for opening. Pulling chairs from the tables, I moved around the room before giving each table one more wipe down. By the time I'd finished, members of Bones MC started arriving. They always arrived about an hour before the bar opened. It was why I started coming in early. To get the bar ready for the club.

The Boneyard was owned by the club. As bars went, I suppose it was decent enough. A little rough, but the guys in the club usually kept a handle on things. I did my best to not interact unless I had to. As a result, I think most of the guys thought it would take too much effort to get me to loosen up. And really, I wasn't much of a catch. They probably all knew my past and had no interest in getting involved. Which was fine by me. I just wanted to save enough money to get an apartment not in a motel. And maybe have a cat.

Once the boys started filing in, I lost myself in work. Trying to keep drinks straight. Keeping the tables clean. Dodging hands of patrons. I hated being touched. That came from prison. The only time people touched was to hurt.

"Get a move on, girl!" A large man with a thick, chest-length beard and a bald head snapped at me when I didn't immediately bring his beer. He was here at least three times a week. Always, he harassed me. He wasn't overt about it, and he always stayed away from the bar and Pops and as many of the Bones men as he could.

When I returned with his drink, I set it down in front of him and turned to leave. He grabbed my arm and pulled me back around. The instant he touched me, it felt like my skin was crawling. Everything inside me rebelled at the contact. His hand hurt my arm, his strength bruising my flesh. I had to bite my lip to keep from giving him the satisfaction of crying out.

"When I tell you I want something, you drop everything else and get it! You get me?"

"Let me go," I said levelly. Inside I was screaming. I wanted to jerk away, to run as hard as I could in the other direction. But I knew from experience that fighting back when I couldn't win would only encourage a bully. I should have kept silent, but I hated his touch so much, the words slipped out before I could stop them.

He sneered at me. "I'll let you go when I'm damned well good and ready." He pulled me roughly to him. Even sitting, he was nearly as tall as I was. And probably two hundred pounds heavier. "Little whore. You been teasin' me since the first time you saw me. Tonight, you're gonna put out."

"Let me go. Now." That was another thing I'd learned in prison. You put up or shut up. Once I'd set a boundary, I had to follow through or this would never end. And this guy would get what he wanted.

He squeezed my arm harder, this time standing and pulling me against him. "You'll get under that fuckin' table and suck my fuckin' dick like the good little whore you are, or I'll carry you outta here and we'll all have a fuckin' go."

His buddies laughed and clinked beer bottles like it was one big party. There was no way I could keep these guys from doing whatever they wanted unless someone came to my rescue. Which this guy had obviously planned for. It was a dark corner fairly close to the door. All he had to do was get me outside before anyone noticed. Assuming anyone cared. But I had the feeling the guys from Bones might take exception to anyone outside their territory taking an employee out of their bar. That's the way it was in prison. Bones may not claim me as one of their own, but they would absolutely not allow another gang to disrupt their business or mess with their employees. At least, that's what I was counting on.

The second the words were out of his mouth, my hand shot between his legs and grabbed his crotch. I squeezed his balls as hard as I could, thankful he'd grabbed my left arm and not my right. He gave a strangled cry and doubled over, letting go of my arm, trying to pry my fingers loose but unable to do more than weakly tug at my wrist. I squeezed just that little bit tighter, putting every ounce of strength I had into hanging on and tugging with a sharp jerk. The big guy fell to his knees and I let go, stepping back quickly. I gripped my heavy serving tray in both hands, bringing it back like I was readying myself to hit him with it even as I continued to back away.

I bumped into someone and a big palm landed on my shoulder. I thought I was in big trouble, but the hand pulled me back gently, and a huge guy stepped in front of me, putting himself between me and the three men at the table.

"There a problem here?"

"Yeah, there's a fuckin' problem! Bitch threw herself at me then tried to back out. Tried to crush my fuckin' balls for no fuckin' reason!"

"In my experience, women like Cotton don't put their hands on men like you willingly." Oh, my God! Could this night get any worse? The man who'd come to my rescue was Chase Dutton. I knew he was a member of Bones, but I tried to stay away from him as much as I could. It was no secret his brother was a police officer and the last thing I wanted was to have another set of eyes on me. I had no idea why Pops and Cain had hired me, but I didn't want any complications in case they changed their mind.

"Why, you son of a bitch!"

The big guy lunged at Chase, but Chase simply caught him by the throat, pulling a gun and bringing it to the man's temple in one smooth move. The second the barrel touched his head, Chase cocked it.

"No one touches the servers. Especially when they don't want it."

"But she --" He was cut off when Chase brought the butt of the gun down on his head once before putting the barrel back to his temple. The guy's knees threatened to buckle, but he kept his footing. Barely.

"Don't matter if she did. When you touched her, she changed her mind. That's all that counts. So you and your buddies here are all gonna fuckin' leave the bar. Now. Don't come back."

"You can't throw us out!" One of his buddies had stood but made no move to get help. In fact, he had his hands up and backed up a couple steps, belying his statement.

"He can," Pops said, coming up behind me. Again, he moved me gently out of the way, putting himself between me and the three men. "So can I. We both say to get the fuck out."

The bar had gone quiet near us, but the other side seemed oblivious. I looked around to see a couple of patrons at my tables raising nearly empty glasses or bottles wanting refills. I desperately wanted to duck my head and just go on about my job, but I had no idea what was expected of me.

"You good, Cotton?" Chase asked, not looking back at me but still eyeing the men who'd yet to leave.

"Yes," I said softly. Automatically. My arm hurt, but I wasn't about to draw more attention to myself. "May I go back to work?"

He glanced at me then and I quickly looked away. Chase Dutton was the sexiest man I'd ever seen. And a man I had no business even looking at. He also seemed to hate me on sight. Cain and Pops both assured me they would keep my incarceration to themselves, and I didn't want to take a chance on anyone else finding out. Which Chase likely had. Things always changed when anyone found out. People I thought were friends suddenly wanted nothing to do with me. I couldn't really blame them, but it hurt that no one thought me important enough to find out my side of the story. I'd kind of been crushing on Chase from a distance, and to have him affirm that I wasn't worth befriending -- even though I already knew that's what he thought -- would hurt worse than when it had happened before. Because I was stupid to let my emotions get the better of me like this.

"What?" Chase glanced back at me, then snapped, "No you can't go back to work! Get your ass to the office! I'll talk to you after I've taken out the trash over here."

The big guy snickered, but Chase just hit him in the butt of his gun again, this time in the face. "Next sound you make is a bullet to the kneecap."

"Go on, girl," Pops said, urging me back toward the bar and the office behind it. "We'll be there once this is done."

I nodded, my whole body trembling. Tears threatened to fall but I held them back by sheer force of will. I would not cry in the middle of a biker bar. I just wouldn't!

Hurrying around the people, I placed my tray at the edge of the bar and headed back to the locker room. No way I was sticking around just to get fired. Not for the first time, I wished I had a car, though not just to get to work quicker. I wanted to make a clean getaway. No way anyone followed me. Pops especially would probably be glad to be rid of me.

I'd just shrugged into my still wet backpack when a decidedly irritated, masculine voice cut through the noise coming from the bar. "Just where the fuck do you think you're going?"

I turned, knowing I was going to have to face Chase after all. Wincing, I met his gaze for a brief moment before looking away. "Look, I'm just saving you and Pops the trouble of firing me. It won't look good for my… uh… resume?"

He crossed his arms over a strong, wide chest as he gave a derisive snort. "Resume, huh."

"Yeah. My resume. Believe it or not, I'll be looking for a job the second I leave here."

"No one said you were getting fired, Cotton." He sighed, scrubbing a hand over his face then the back of his neck. "Now, get your ass in the office. We need to talk about what happened."

"Nothing to talk about." I couldn't help my mulish tone. The very last thing in this world I wanted to do was talk with anyone about what had happened. Or why I wanted to keep a low profile.

"Plenty to talk about," he snapped back. "You're not goin' anywhere right now except where I tell you to go. Now, go park your sweet little ass on the fuckin' couch in my office. I'll be there in a minute with Pops."

"You're not the boss of me!"

He snorted again. "Keep tellin' yourself that, Cotton." Then he jerked his head in the direction he wanted me to go. Wouldn't you know it, my stupid feet shuffled off in that same direction.

Chapter Two

Chase

God as my witness, I tried my fucking hardest to leave Cotton alone. The poor girl just screamed "battered woman," but I got the feeling it wasn't from a past relationship. Especially with how she reacted to Butch. The three men used to belong to Scars and Bars MC before we got rid of that lot. As far as I knew, they were the only three left in the city. Instead of reacting with fear, Cotton had taken an aggressive approach. Almost like she wanted to make sure the rest of them knew not to fuck with her.

She was like some kind of angel. Pale blonde hair that was nearly platinum, a slight but strong frame, and gently rounded breasts and hips belied the hardness in her eyes. She tried hard to hide it, but this girl had known violence. Had probably even killed. But probably not more than once and I was sure she'd had a good reason.

I watched her flounce off into the office I'd set up for me and Pops. Cain had turned over the day-to-day running of the Boneyard to us. Pops because he'd always been there and refused to quit helping. Me because I'd needed something to occupy my mind so the nightmares of shit I'd done didn't overwhelm me. And yeah, it had taken a lot of hair on my balls to admit that to Cain. Though I never hesitated to kill or torture when the occasion called for it, the outfit I'd been working in when Bones found me hadn't always given my team the correct information. As a result, I had to wonder how many of the people I'd hurt had been innocents just caught in a bad situation. It kept me up at night. All the fucking time.

Walking in behind Cotton, I shut the door and

sat behind my desk. "I don't fuckin' need this," I muttered.

"I told you I'd just go," Cotton said softly. "It'll save you paperwork."

"This isn't about firing you, Cotton." I snapped harshly at the poor girl when I was really mad at myself. I took a breath. "Are you all right? Did that bastard hurt you?"

"I'm fine," she said softly, though she rubbed her left upper arm absently. It was where Butch had grabbed her.

"Let me see your arm."

"I said it's fine." She finally looked up at me. "Can I go now?"

"No. I'm not done." She grumbled something and looked away, but sat still. "Where you stayin', Cotton?"

"The motel. Same as I was when I started."

"You got wheels?" She shook her head. I half thought she'd lie, but one thing I'd noticed about Cotton was that she didn't lie. At least, not to anyone in the club. "I'll have Cain set you up in the clubhouse. There's plenty of room and there will always be someone there to give you a ride to work."

"You don't have to do that. I don't want to put anyone out."

"You ain't. That place you're stayin' at ain't safe and there are all kinds of drug deals goin' on there. God only knows what else."

"Yeah," she muttered. "Noticed that."

I sighed. This wasn't going as smoothly as I'd hoped. Though, I'd picked a piss poor time to bring this up with her. "Tell me what's goin' on, Cotton. You runnin' from somebody?"

"No," she said with a little shake of her head.

"I'm just trying to get by's all." She looked away before taking a breath and continuing. "Look. I need this job. I wouldn't be here otherwise."

"I get that. What I don't get is how someone as good at servin' as you are ain't workin' somewhere in town where fuckin' bastards like Butch and his buddies can't corner you and threaten you. You never get orders wrong, you're attentive to all the customers, not just your own. I've seen you helping out when other girls get behind. You could make way more in tips at restaurants instead of a fuckin' biker bar."

I thought she might be going to answer me, then she got that mulish look on her face and shook her head once, clamping her lips firmly together. We stared at each other for a long while, neither budging.

"Fine," I said. "But I'll get it out of you sooner or later. Bettin' Cain knows."

She gasped, her arms which had been crossed in over her breasts, loosened and she pushed herself off the couch as she stood to face me. "He promised he wouldn't tell anyone."

"Then tell me yourself so I don't have to ask him."

"It's none of your business! He knows my past and hired me anyway. I'm just supposed to tell him if there are any problems."

"Well, I'd classify Butch as a problem. I'll take you to Cain and you can let him know what went down today."

I could tell the exact moment she knew I had her and had to suppress a triumphant grin. Instead, I stood and crossed to the door. "Shall we?"

"I can go to him myself. I don't need you tattling and trying to babysit me."

"We can discuss gettin' you settled in the

clubhouse while we're at it," I continued smoothly, ignoring her protests. I let her precede me out the door, then guided her outside the bar to my truck. I hated driving the thing, but the rain was torrential. Riding the bike wasn't an option tonight.

I unlocked the door and stood there while Cotton climbed up into the cab. "Put on your seatbelt," I said before shutting the door again and trotting around the front of the truck. Rain was still pouring. Once inside, I shook out my hair before pushing the button to start the truck. "Once we claim a room for you, we'll go get your stuff from the motel. But we're moving you out of there tonight."

"You can't just take over my life, you know. I don't belong to your club."

"You're an employee at our bar. That makes you our responsibility."

"I see," she said softly. "Trust me when I say I have way more to lose than you so if I fuck up so there's no reason for you to be concerned I'll do something to damage your club's reputation or whatever."

I wanted to strangle the beautiful girl. And wrap her up in my arms and protect her from everything. I had no idea what was going on, but it was time to find out. And I would. If she wouldn't tell me, I'd lean on Cain and Pops. Because there was no way Pops didn't know. No one in Bones had secrets from Mama and Pops. I'd argue that they knew more about our members than even Cain to a certain extent. Either way, I'd find out today. Why? I wish I had a reason why I needed this. All I could come up with was that Cotton was mine. I hadn't had any interactions with her, had no idea of her secrets. But I wanted the woman with a fierceness I had never experienced before. There was no letting her go.

The trip to the clubhouse was only a few minutes. In that time, Cotton didn't look at me once. Instead, she turned her head away, looking out the passenger window. Her hands were clasped tightly around the ratty backpack she carried.

I pulled into the garage attached to the main clubhouse. It was where most of us kept our vehicles, especially if we were at a party or meeting. While I wanted Cotton to feel comfortable, I wanted her close. With the addition of a few newly patched members and prospects to the club, I knew space had to be pretty tight. It was why Cain had ordered homes be built around the main complex creating a wider community in our own private space. A few houses were completed, with several more being set up when the club had simply bought new mobile homes to get a fast start on building our neighborhood.

"This isn't a bad thing, Cotton," I said as I turned off the truck and turned to face her. "You need a safe place to stay and we can provide that."

"Yeah? And exactly what will I be expected to do in return for the housing? Because I know everyone here earns their keep. I also hear the girls in the club talking when they come into the bar. I'm not anyone's whore."

"Babe, relax. Ain't nobody gonna ask you to do anything you don't want to do. Bones takes care of our own."

"Well, I ain't a club girl or whatever. I ain't a member of your club either, Chase. Don't need help from anyone." She added the last part under her breath like she hadn't really meant me to hear her.

"Let's just go talk to Cain. Angel will be there and she'll look out for you."

"Who's Angel?"

"Cain's ol' lady. She's a good woman."

"In my experience, wives and girlfriends aren't exactly looking out for other women in their gang. They're seen as competition and I'm most definitely not interested in putting myself in that kind of position."

I stared hard at her for several seconds. I could see she was struggling with this. She was nervous. Sweat dotted her upper lip and she fidgeted in her seat. Finally, I just sighed. Only one way to prove to her we only wanted to help her. Well, the club only wanted that. I wanted more than she was ready to give just yet. I'd get her there, though.

"You've been around us long enough to know the difference between an MC and a gang, baby." I reached over and squeezed her hand briefly. The contact sent a jolt of pleasure through me. She gasped, her eyes widening before she looked away again, a becoming blush stealing up her neck and face. Yeah. She'd felt it too. I promised myself then I'd make sure I touched her often. "Come on. You have to tell Cain what happened at the bar anyway. If you ain't satisfied with his reaction or anything about the meeting, you don't have to stay here. But I urge you to give us the benefit of the doubt. We're not into hurting women and children. We try our best to help."

With a sigh, Cotton closed her eyes and nodded. "I can do that," she said softly. Did I imagine she winced? "It's the least I can do for Cain and Pops giving me the job at the Boneyard in the first place. Guess I'm doing exactly what I don't like people doing to me." That got my attention. But now wasn't the time to call her out on it.

Once we were walking toward the clubhouse, I

snagged Cotton's hand. I thought she'd tug it away, but instead, she clung tightly. I could feel a slight trembling in her hand and her palm was slightly sweaty. There had to be more to this than simple nerves. This girl was scared. Of us? But if she was that afraid of us, why work at the Boneyard?

I was pondering this as I gave her a covert glance. Her head was up. Her chin out. To outward appearances, she was walking calmly beside me. There was a purpose to her gait but also a hint of... something? Defiance didn't seem to be the correct term. She wasn't defiant, but not resigned. It was like anywhere she was going was her own decision and no one was going to make it for her. Even if she wanted to be anywhere other than where she was. It was time to get to the bottom of this.

Cain stepped from the hallway into the great room, Angel at his side with her hand in his. They glanced around the room until Angel spotted me. She threw up her hand and smiled in greeting as we approached.

"It's good to see you, Chase," she said warmly, then addressed Cotton with the same welcoming smile. "You must be Cotton. I'm so glad to finally meet you. I've seen you at the Boneyard but haven't had the chance to speak with you. You're always working so hard I hate to distract you."

"You're doing a fantastic job, Cotton," Cain said. "We're glad to have you with us." Cain could be abrasive on the best of days, but he was gentle with Cotton. That got my back up when I should have been grateful. I knew that one harsh word in the wrong direction and Cotton would bolt.

"Thank you," she said softly, not looking up at either Cain or Angel.

"Can we go to your office?" I asked.

Cain nodded and jerked his head in that direction, but not before a pointed look at mine and Cotton's joined hands. He didn't say anything, but raised an eyebrow. I just shook my head slightly and followed him down the hall.

Once inside the quiet confines of Cain's office, he sat behind his desk and pulled Angel onto his lap. The woman protested slightly, but when his arms came around her, Angel's expression softened and she allowed the intimate contact with her husband.

"Now. What can we do for you?" Despite the fact that his woman was curled in his lap, Cain's demeanor was all business.

Cotton snatched her hand from mine and her eyes got wide in panic. She looked ready to bolt.

"Don't worry," Angel said to Cotton. "You're safe here."

"I know that, but..." She trailed off, looking at Cain, then ducking her head. Frustration and shame radiated from her like a neon sign.

"I told you I didn't keep secrets from my woman," Cain said softly. "Other than her and Pops, no one in this club knows anything you didn't tell them."

Cotton closed her eyes, one errant tear tracking down her cheek. I wanted to pull her to me and kiss away that tear but there was no way she'd allow that. Hell, there was no way I should feel that way but this woman pulled at something inside me. I had no hope of resisting her. Maybe she was what I needed in my life to atone for my sins in the past. Quieting her demons might take the edge off my guilt. But, really, what right did I have to pull her into my problems and use her for my own end? No. It was more than that, but I wasn't ready to admit it just yet. Not even to myself.

"I had some trouble at the bar tonight." Cotton spoke the words softly and not looking up from where her hands now twisted in her lap.

"Are you OK?" Cain asked. This time, his voice had the edge I'd come to expect from the older man. Cotton's face tightened, but that was the only indication she registered the change in his tone.

"Yes."

Cain looked at me for confirmation. I stretched out my legs, crossing them at the ankles and putting my arm over the back of the couch behind Cotton's shoulders. My thumb grazed over her shoulder gently several times before I answered.

"I suspect she may have some bruising on her arm where Butch grabbed her, but I intervened before things went too badly."

"Butch," Cain snapped. "Fuckin' scum. That bunch needs to get a fuckin' clue and leave before we have to help the last of 'em have a fuckin' accident."

"Cain," Angel chided softly. "She came to you with this like you told her to."

"Yeah. I'm sorry, Cotton. One would have thought I'd've learned my lesson."

Angel snorted. "You're a guy. Men never learn without reminders."

"I'll spank your ass for that later," Cain chuckled before leaning in to kiss Angel softly on the lips. I had no idea if the byplay was intentional or not, but the easy show of affection, along with the fact that Angel was the one to calm Cain when he was the president of Bones and Cotton probably expected him to defer to no one, seemed to ease the tension in Cotton's shoulders.

"Tell me what happened." Cain brought his full

attention back to Cotton.

She relayed her version of events. The longer she talked the more tense she became until it was easy to tell she was near tears. "Am I going to have to leave now?" Her voice was tremulous when I knew she tried hard not to show any emotion.

"No," Cain and Angel answered at the same time. Cain leaned in and kissed Angel's temple before continuing. "No, Cotton. You ain't leavin'. None of that was your fault, and even if it was we wouldn't just toss you out on your ear. We'll take care of Butch and the rest of those leftovers from Scars and Bars. That's on me for not puttin' a stop to those bastards comin' in the bar a long time ago. Now. Chase says you need a place to crash."

"No. I've got a place."

"You ain't stayin' in that motel another fuckin' night, Cotton." I dropped my arm from the back of the couch to drape over her shoulders. She stiffened but allowed the contact. Cain chuckled.

"She know you're claimin' her, Chase? Because I kinda don't think she does."

Cotton gasped, looking up at me. "What does that mean? I told you I wasn't gonna be nobody's whore!"

"Relax, honey," Angel said, sliding from Cain's lap and going to Cotton. She knelt in front of Cotton like she might while soothing a child. "That's not what he means."

"Then what does he mean?" Cotton gave me a fierce look, trying to scoot away from me, but I just pulled her back.

"It means he's going to take care of you. Make sure you have everything you need and are protected. He won't let any of the brothers hit on you and it will make the riffraff at the bar think twice about harassing you. That's all."

"For now," I muttered. Angel shot me an exasperated look.

"No one at the club bothers me except Butch and his bunch."

"They've done this before? Why didn't you say anything?" I wasn't sure what made me angrier. The fact that I hadn't noticed she was in trouble or that she'd kept it from me and Pops.

"Every night since I got there." She sounded small. Afraid. Miserable. "This isn't going to work out, is it?"

"Why would you say that?" I glanced sharply at Cain. "I want to know what's going on. Since I'm manager of the Boneyard, I think I need to know."

Cain just sat back, crossing one leg over his knee. He grinned as he spoke. "You need to know what I tell you you need to know. I made a promise to Cotton and I'm not breaking it. You want to know? I suggest you convince Cotton to trust you with her secrets."

Cotton gasped, sitting up straighter. "You mean, you're not going to tell him?"

"We don't break promises, Cotton," Angel said gently. "Not unless it's absolutely necessary and we'd tell you we were going to do it."

"I suppose it's not unreasonable for him to want to know," she said, looking even more miserable but also resigned. "But I don't want…"

"No one's going to think less of you, honey," Angel soothed. "It's your past. No one else's. If you don't want to tell him, don't. Just know that if you couldn't trust Chase, he wouldn't be part of Bones. It's part of their code."

"Maybe…" she swallowed. "Maybe I'll wait a

little bit."

"You'll tell me when you're ready." I tightened my arm around her and leaned in to kiss her temple. She looked up at me, confusion warring with a yearning so intense it nearly broke me. My chest ached for this woman, even without knowing her story. It was obvious she wanted social interaction but was afraid to put herself out there for whatever reason. I also thought she wanted me as much as I wanted her.

"Maybe." Her voice was barely above a whisper and she looked away from me.

"In the meantime," Cain said. "We'll set you up with a room in the clubhouse. As is usual with us whenever one of our members needs to coax his woman into trusting him with her heart, we just happen to have a room available next to Chase's."

"We'll need to get her things from the motel," I said. "I don't want her going back."

"Not a problem. Have Daniel, Cliff, and Deadeye go with you. That should be enough to make anyone wanting to cause trouble to think twice." Cain sent off a quick text. When his phone buzzed he gave a satisfied nod. "They'll meet you in the garage."

"I can do this myself," Cotton muttered. "Seems a bit overkill to send four guys with me to get one backpack full of stuff."

"We take the safety of our own seriously, honey," Angel said smoothly. "That includes you. Besides, it makes the boys feel needed and wanted. We have to keep their fragile egos intact."

"Come on," I said. "Let's get this done and get back here. We'll get you settled then you and I can have a talk."

She glanced up at me, looking equal parts resigned and defiant. "I don't see there's anything to talk about."

"Plenty to talk about."

"Can't you just take me back to the bar? When we left, it put Pops down a server."

"Already taken care of," I said.

"I'll need to... uh..." She looked up helplessly at Cain. "You know. Notify..."

"I'll take care of that," Cain said. "Just check in with them tomorrow. It's all good."

"My life hasn't been good for more than ten years," she said softly.

"It will get better," Angel said, giving her a hug. "I promise, it will get better."

Chapter Three

Cotton

Chase led me back through the common room where the party was in full swing. All around were naked and partially naked women. Several of the guys threw up hands at Chase as we walked. Several of the women, too. Chase acknowledged the men, ignored the women, and kept a firm grip on my hand as if to keep me from twisting free of him. I'm not too ashamed to admit I clung to his hand. I had never welcomed the advances of men. To do so meant to open myself up to attack. Chase felt different. Had from the first day I saw him. Maybe it was my attraction to him. But when we entered that room full of strange or mostly strange men, my first instinct had been to stay close to him. He'd protect me and never take advantage of me. I had absolutely no reason to believe that, but I did.

As we walked, three more guys fell into step behind us. I recognized Deadeye. In his late forties, the man frequented the Boneyard. The other two men were younger, and I'd never seen them before.

Once out of the clubhouse and away from the noise, Chase introduced us. "I know you've met Deadeye at the bar. Cliff and Daniel are Cain's adopted sons and prospects with Bones. They also work at ExFil with us as well."

"ExFil?" That wasn't a name that made any sense to me.

"It's a paramilitary organization Cain owns," Chase explained. "We run ops all over the world for various countries, including the U.S. Cliff was a Marine while Daniel was a Navy SEAL."

"Seems several of your club have been in the

military. Has everyone?"

"Mostly. There are a few who weren't, but everyone has their own talents and training they bring to the club. Even a few of the ol' ladies work for us."

"I didn't expect that," I responded softly. "Seems like these types of clubs are very male dominate."

"One of our members, Shadow's woman, Millie, has a sister who is a trained assassin. Millie's just as deadly as Venus and is prospecting for us. She'll probably make a patched member if she wants it."

"Yeah," Daniel said with a chuckle. "Likely before either me or Daniel and we grew up here."

Cliff took up the narrative. "Millie's a tiny little thing, but don't let that fool you. She could probably kick the asses of every member of Bones. And her sister is even worse."

"Cliff's right. You don't wanna mess with Venus or Millie."

The two brothers seemed good natured and oddly proud of the women they spoke of. Like they were little sisters or something when it was obvious they didn't consider themselves as skilled a fighter as either of the women. And these men were military? Definitely not what I was used to.

Chase started up the truck as we all climbed in. The second we were on the road, Chase reached over and took my hand again. For some stupid reason, I let him. I knew better than this. Letting him get close to me would only invite heartache when he found out about my past. And I knew it was just a matter of time. Probably just the time it took to get my shit and get back to the clubhouse. I knew without a doubt Chase would have my secrets tonight.

In a way, I was almost relieved. Sure, I was frightened. I didn't want him to look at me differently, but it would also mean I had no secrets from him. He'd see me at my worst and maybe, just maybe, he could see past it and still want to hold my hand as we walked across a roomful of men at his clubhouse.

It took all of ten minutes for me to gather my meager belongings and stuff them into my backpack. Chase was silent the whole time, standing with his back to the closed door of my room like a solid boulder. His jaw clenched and I realized he was upset about something. The last thing I wanted was to put him out when he'd been kind.

"You didn't have to come with me, you know." It was the only thing I could think of that would put him in a bad mood. Maybe he wanted to get back to the bar. Or maybe it was the party. Lord knew there was plenty of entertainment from what I saw. I doubted there was a woman in the place who wouldn't volunteer to make his evening more enjoyable than I was right now.

"I know." It was all he said, watching me intently.

"That's it. That's everything."

Again, his jaw clenched. I ignored him and put my backpack over my shoulders.

Chase and I stepped out of the second floor room onto the outside balcony walkway. We'd taken two steps when a hulking figure emerged from a doorway and swung a bat straight at Chase's head.

Chase realized just in time and blocked the bat with his hand, catching it with a loud *smack* that had to have hurt. If it did, Chase didn't show it. He yanked the bat away from his attacker, throwing it over the railing. Two more men came at us with yells, one grabbed me, clamping an arm around my neck and backing away several feet while the other two fought Chase.

His arm was so tight, I clutched at it, just trying to drag in a breath. I was short and this guy was way taller than me. When he backed us away from Chase, he lifted me off my feet. By my head. I kicked and fought as hard as I could. Unable to scream, I knew I was on my own.

One of my kicks must have caught something important, because the breath left the guy's lungs in a putrid fume. His hold lessened and I was able to slide under his arm, freeing my neck and letting me drag in a breath of air. But the fight wasn't over. I knew better than to sit there just breathing. Looking up, I saw the guy bent double, clutching his groin. I scrambled to my back and kicked out, catching him in the nose with enough force to send blood flying.

The big bastard fell backward, smacking his head on the concrete when he landed. Immediately, I was on my feet, turning back to Chase where I knew he fought against at least two opponents.

The fight was pretty one sided. Chase, though outnumbered, was a hell of a fighter. He quickly snapped the arm of one of the men before taking out the other one's leg. Howls of pain echoed in the night, prompting doors to open down the line. No one offered to help or call the cops. Like I expected it in this place. Most everyone here was into some kind of petty illegal activity. What was one more fight to them? It would be more likely someone would be taking bets on the winner.

Just as Chase gave a vicious kick to the thigh of the man still trying to fight despite his knee injury, two more men joined the fray. I ducked into the doorway and out of the way of the men fighting. I was about to run for the help I knew waited for us in the truck when I realized it was Cliff and Deadeye who'd stepped in.

Cliff put himself between me and the other men while Deadeye engaged the last man.

I shouldn't have worried. Deadeye and Cliff were on the landing helping Chase while Daniel pulled the truck around to the stairs, ready for us to climb in and get the hell out of there. The second the truck came into view, Cliff urged me in that direction while the other men finished. I resisted, not wanting to leave Chase behind even though Deadeye was the much better choice to have his back if things got worse.

It was only then that I recognized the three men who'd attacked us. Butch and his buddies from the bar. Chase wasn't even winded. He leaned down to Butch. The man's right leg was at two odd angles. One above and one below his knee. No doubt the break was extensive and wicked.

"Next time I see you motherfuckers in this town is the day you fuckin' die." This was a side of Chase I'd only caught glimpses of before. He was a straight up killer in that moment. I had the distinct feeling that the only reason he let Butch live was because there was a handful of witnesses to what was going on. Somewhere, there might even be someone recording the fight to post to social media. Seemed the thing people did nowadays.

Without another word, Chase wrapped his arm around me and hurried me down the stairs and into the truck. Seconds later, we peeled out of the parking lot and headed back to the Bones clubhouse.

"You OK?" Chase still had his arm around me and pulled me closer to him as we sped down the road.

"Yeah. Just… shaken up. I'd almost forgotten I still needed to pay close attention to my surroundings. I should have seen Butch."

"That's not on you, baby," Chase said. I looked

up at him and, though his gaze was straight ahead, I could still see the anger in his chiseled features. "That was all me. My fault all the way around."

"That's what we were there for," Deadeye said. "We had your back. You had Cotton to worry about. We worried about you." The big man shrugged. "Besides, even though they had the drop on you, you still beat the piss out of 'em. You didn't need us."

"They had Cotton," Chase insisted. "I owe you guys. Big time."

"Give your girl some credit," Cliff said. "She held her own. Good thinking to go to your back and use your leg strength, by the way." Cliff turned around from his position in the front passenger seat and grinned at me. "You decide to toss Chase to the curb, you come see me. You can fight at my side anytime."

"Not the time, Cliff," Chase growled. Cliff just chuckled, not in the least bit intimidated by the larger man. I thought perhaps he should have been if the look on Chase's face was any indication, though I had no idea why. Cliff was practically offering to take me off Chase's hands. If he was angry because he had to babysit me, this was the perfect opportunity to get rid of me.

"Thanks, Cliff," I said softly. "And thanks to you, Daniel, and Deadeye for coming for us."

Deadeye nodded once, then looked out the window again. Cliff winked again. "Anytime, babe."

The rest of the ride was spent in silence. I knew once we got back and in my room I'd have to come clean with Chase. With his brother being a cop, I doubted this was going to end well for me. But after seeing the worst humanity had to offer me in prison -- both the inmates and the guards -- I swore I'd do my best to at least be honest and keep my word. It was really all I had left of my dignity. Honesty and integrity. It was all I had to offer anyone in my life now.

Chase was out of the truck almost before it stopped moving, pulling me after him. He hurried us around the side of the clubhouse, not through the front like he'd taken me before. His strides were long and I had to jog to keep up with his pace. When I tripped and stumbled, he turned to me, looking even more angry than before.

"Christ," he bit out. Then scooped me up in his arms and headed up the stairs. Even with my weight he took them two at a time, brushing past women in the hallway without even acknowledging their presence. More than one man called out a greeting but Chase only grunted. I thought I heard laughter but it was hard to say.

Finally, he set me down in front of a door nearly at the end of the hall. He unlocked it then dragged me inside with him. Slamming the door shut, he locked it but didn't turn back around to face me. Instead, he braced both hands on the door and banged his head against it several times.

I took several steps away from him, but didn't turn my back on him. I'd seen enough people on the edge to know that, for some reason, Chase had reached his limit. Arguing with him or pushing against him wasn't a good idea right now. Instead, I just stood where I was, ready to sprint away from him if necessary but knowing in my heart he'd never hurt me. Not like that. He'd have just fired me and told me to never come back. No. There was something else going on inside Chase that I had no hope of understanding unless he chose to share it with me.

"Put your things in the bedroom," he said softly.

"Just put your pack on the bed and come sit on the couch with me." He didn't turn around, but I didn't need to see his face to know this was an order pure and simple. I hurried to obey him.

Assuming the only door in the place was the bedroom, I hurried through it and did as instructed. The suite wasn't overly large, but it made good use of space. The main room was a combination kitchen and living room, while the bedroom had the only bathroom. Again, not large, the bedroom had a king-size bed, a dresser, and what I assumed was a closet with folding doors. Everything was neat and clean. Nothing out of place.

Not wanting to keep him waiting when I had no idea of his current mental state, I hurried back into the living room and shut the door to the bedroom. He was already waiting for me on the couch.

Chase Dutton was brutally handsome. His short, full beard only accentuated his masculine features. It was gray at the chin, but was salt and pepper over his cheeks as well as his short-cropped hair. Unlike many of the men in Bones, Chase only sported a few tattoos, most of which looked like service tattoos, though I hadn't had the pleasure of examining them closely. Tall, heavily muscled, he was the epitome of strength and power. I'd been in such a weak position for the last ten years, so he was the very last man I should be attracted to unless he'd given me an unbreakable promise to always be my protector. He hadn't. But in my mind, he was. I had no hope of fighting my attraction for him, and having him taken an interest in me this evening had only cemented my feelings. To put it bluntly, I was fucking fucked.

"Come sit with me," he said softly, reaching out a hand for me. He seemed to have calmed down somewhat, but there was still an edge about him I didn't like.

"Are you angry with me? Am I in trouble?" I needed to know where I stood before putting myself in too close a proximity to him. I doubted I could get to the door and unlock it before he could get to me if he proved to be a threat, but I needed to know what was going on.

Chase sighed, scrubbing a hand over his face. "No, honey. It's not you. I should have been more careful taking you back to that motel. I'm angry at myself. I made a rookie mistake."

I shrugged. "Everyone makes mistakes. But that wasn't your fault. If I'd --"

"If you'd what?" The fierce look he gave me made me back up a step before I realized I'd done it. "If you'd done what Butch had wanted you to in the bar? If you'd not fought against him when he manhandled you? No, Cotton. That's not something to even contemplate." I knew Chase wasn't going to hurt me, but I stood there trembling anyway. Years of being so powerless -- some of it my own choice -- had conditioned me to expect to get hurt. This man might be capable of violence, but he was first and foremost a protector. He wouldn't intentionally harm someone weaker than him. Even if they deserved it.

Closing his eyes, Chase took a deep, calming breath. When he opened his eyes, he was more in control again. He held his hand out once again, but didn't say anything. After several seconds, I stepped toward him and took his hand and let him tug me to sit on the couch.

"We have things to discuss," he said. "First of all, there's been a change of plans. You're going to stay here. With me. I know I said you'd have your own space, but I can't do that right now. So you're stuck with me."

"It's fine. I know it was short notice."

"It's not that, Cotton," he said. "I need you close. Those bastards nearly got their hands on you and I'm not going to get over that anytime soon. I want you where I know you're safe and comfortable."

"Would some of the other guys here hurt me?" I was more than a little confused. Had I misjudged all of them? I thought they were decent guys. Everyone I'd met had treated me kindly, but if they were like some of the women in prison had told me, maybe it was all a facade.

"Not at all, honey. No one here would ever harm you. The club girls sometimes get aggressive, but not to the point of really hurting you. And they know to keep their distance."

"Then why…"

"We'll get to that later. You're not ready to hear it and I'm not ready to share. Now. You have secrets. I want them. Now."

Annoyed at his attitude, I sat back, crossing my arms over my chest. "Not liking your tone, Chase. My secrets are my own. The only reason I told Cain and Pops was because I wanted a job at the Boneyard."

"Then tell me for the same reason."

"I've already got a job there. Why would I go over all this again?"

"Because you want to tell me. You tell me your past. I'll tell you mine. And I promise, my past will rival yours."

"You think so?"

"Wanna bet?" There was something in his eyes that told me he was only half teasing. But he'd intrigued me. Not because I thought we were going to play a game of who's the better killer. I had no doubt the man before me was as deadly as they came. In fact, I'd bet my life the man had killed more than once. There was something in his eyes. I'd learned the look in prison. I could always tell which of the female prisoners and which guards had killed because they all had that same look in their eyes. I couldn't describe it, but I saw it reflected back at me every time I looked into the mirror.

Despite myself, I found he'd drawn me into the wicked game. "What's the stakes?"

"Winner's choice."

I knew this was a bad idea. But he'd piqued my interest now. "Fine. You go first." I had to make sure to get in. If I was doing this, I wasn't starting.

"OK." He reached for my hands, clasping them firmly in both of his. "Before I joined ExFil and Bones, I was an assassin."

Chapter Four

Chase

It seemed to take Cotton several seconds to process what I'd said. Still another few to believe she'd heard me right. Then she swallowed.

"You're not kidding, are you." She made it a statement. Oddly enough, her hands tightened around mine. I think I was expecting her to reject me. To push me away. Instead, she seemed to cling to me even more. It was a huge gamble on my part, but I could tell I'd made the right choice.

"No, baby. I'm not. I was part of a group of mercenaries working for a really shady organization. There are a lot of things I still don't know. I'd been hand-picked for my skills but mostly for my level headedness and my ability to do the hard jobs. Even when I didn't want to. I was assured that we were working for the greater good. There were certain very strict protocols in place to assure my team any target we were sent after deserved the justice they were getting. I believed in them. In my team and our team leader. In the end?" I shrugged and shook my head. "I was just another bad guy doing bad things. I almost killed a woman married to one of my brothers here. That's when Cain took me in. He didn't have to, but he listened to my story, fantastical as it was, and believed me. Bones had some friends in high places who knew about my employers. They shut that section down. Some of my team realized how we'd been lied to and manipulated. Others…" I winced even as I remembered. "I executed them. My team. My responsibility. Cain's had my back ever since. Gave me a job with ExFil and a home here."

"Sounds familiar," she muttered. "Cain didn't

hesitate in hiring me, even once he found out everything. I guess he likes taking in strays, huh?" Taking a breath, she began. "I just got out of prison." When she didn't elaborate immediately, I had to stifle my need to tell her to continue. That would have been the exact wrong move. She needed time to tell this in her own way. "Before I go on, I should tell you Cain and Pops read my casefile after requesting it from my parole officer. I gave consent because I never want to deceive people who've given me a chance." She closed her eyes and a single tear tracked down her left cheek. "If you want to read that file, I'll have Cain give it to you."

"I'd rather hear it from you."

She nodded several times, still gripping my hands tightly. Finally, she started. "I killed a man. There were circumstances, but I did it. The guy was the son of a judge in town, so even though the case was taken out of his jurisdiction, I knew there was no way I'd win at trial. My lawyer got the prosecution to accept a deal for manslaughter instead of murder and I took it. I got fifteen years. Served ten of them before I got out on parole."

"Seems a bit excessive to serve that much on a fifteen-year sentence. Did you have a minimum you needed to serve before you were eligible for parole?"

"You would think that, huh? Yeah. I had to serve a quarter of the sentence before being considered for parole. Unfortunately, the parole board doesn't like it when you don't express remorse for your crime. I had none. Told them so."

That made me grin. "That's something I've noticed about you since you've been with us. You don't lie."

"No. It's the one thing I have left that's good

inside me. It may be hard for people to hear. May be hard for me to say. But I won't lie. And I never break a promise." She shrugged. "I guess even murderers have lines they won't cross."

"Somehow, I don't picture you as someone who kills for no reason. There's more to that story."

She gave me a startled look, trying to jerk her hands away but I kept a hold on them. "You... you believe me?"

"Cotton, I know killers. I could see it the first time I laid eyes on you that you'd killed. I could also see the toll it took you. You've killed. But you're not a killer. There's a huge difference. So there had to be a good reason in your mind for you to take that step."

That got more tears from her. Maybe because she hadn't had much kindness in her life and she thought I was being kind to her. She was young. Being in prison that long... yeah. Prison is not kind. She seemed starved for positive attention. I planned on giving it to her in spades.

"The man I killed raped and murdered my older sister. I was hidden. Scared to move. I stayed hidden while he brutalized her and she begged for mercy. Brandon was charged several months later, mainly due to my insistence. I was only thirteen at the time, but the psychiatrist the state had talk to me deemed old enough and mature enough to testify in open court, so I was called before the Grand Jury to see if they thought there was reason enough to charge Brandon and begin building a more solid case against him.

"It was the hardest thing I'd ever had to do. Sitting there looking at that monster. By the time the case finally went to the actual trial, I was fifteen, but it still gave me nightmares afterward." Her breath hitched and her voice cracked, but she continued after a brief pause.

"Anyway. The cross examination was brutal. The defense attorney had me sobbing on the stand before it was over. He basically said I was lying and was trying to get back at Brandon for choosing my sister over me. He was twenty-five years old and I was only thirteen at the time of the event. The jerk even implied I'd killed my sister just to frame Brandon so I got even with both of them.

"In the end, the jury couldn't make a decision. The judge declared a mistrial and found some legal reason to make it so Brandon couldn't be tried again due to double jeopardy. Something about the high probability of my testimony being fabricated and that an innocent young man shouldn't have to be put through this. He said if I continued to defame him in public, Brandon could sue my parents and ruin their lives."

"So he walked away free while you and your parents got dick all."

"Pretty much. By this time, my mother had had some kind of nervous breakdown and was in psychiatric hospital. She was never herself again. My dad drank all the time. I found myself in the position of trying to take care of both of them. My dad blamed me for my mother's mental health. One night, when he was so drunk he could barely talk, he told me if I wanted to make up for everything I'd put his family through, I'd kill that son of a bitch and be done with it." She shrugged. "It had been on my mind since the end of the trial, so…"

"You killed him." My thumbs feathered over her hands where they were still clasped with hers.

"I killed that motherfucker in broad fucking daylight," she said fiercely. The tears started to flow steadily now. It was surreal. She cried, but was steady all the same. Tears continued to course down her face, but she didn't sob, her voice didn't catch, her chin didn't tremble. Those Goddamned tears seemed to release the sorrow and anger inside her in a way she couldn't otherwise manage. "I followed him. Found the perfect place. He was with a bunch of his buddies, in a park near his home. They'd run off all the locals, bullying the ones they could, roughing up the ones who still refused to go. All so they could have the fucking basketball court to themselves." She looked at a point past my shoulder now, seeming to be lost in the past. Those Goddamned tears still leaked in a steady trickle from her eyes. "I watched them for a long while. Out of sight. Just… watching. Listening.

"When Brandon started telling his buddies what he'd done to my sister, bragging about how he'd gotten away with it, how my whole family had been destroyed in one way or another, I just… snapped.

"My father had a Ruger SP101. An older gun, but it was in mint condition and well taken care of. Only fired a few times. I'd done some research and found the best bullet to use in that gun to kill someone, no matter what part of their core body I hit. I loaded it with Critical Defense rounds, and kept it with me at all times. Just waiting for the perfect moment. I think, maybe, I wanted to talk myself out of it? But as the weeks passed, I knew I was long past that."

Cotton let go of my hands with one of hers and swiped at her tears. I wanted to get her some tissue but didn't dare move. It was painfully obvious she needed to get this out. I had to wonder if she'd actually told anyone this version of events or if it had always been glossed over, concealing her feelings in order to just get it over with. She wiped her hand on her jeans and didn't reach for me again. So I reached for her, taking her free hand gently and pulling it back to me. The second I did, her hands tightened on mine in a death grip. She seemed to find the courage inside her to continue, finally looking up at me and meeting my gaze, clinging to me both physically with her hands and emotionally with those shiny, brown eyes.

"I just... walked over to them. I had the gun behind my back, already cocked and ready because I knew there was no way I'd have time to pull the hammer back once I raised it to aim. I deliberately got everything ready to kill Brandon. I used a powerful handgun with bullets that would explode as they entered his body. I made sure it was ready to fire the second I took aim. And I waited until there was no chance of true collateral damage. The mere fact that his buddies stood there and listened to him, laughing as he mimicked how my sister had begged him for her life told me it didn't matter if they got hit because I was a lousy shot or someone knocked my aim off target.

"So I approached them. At first they ignored me. But when I was just close enough I knew there was no way I could miss him entirely, they turned to me. Just as I raised my arm and aimed at Brandon."

Cotton jerked as if remembering the report of the gun as she fired. "The first round went into his chest. The gun was positively deafening as it went off but had surprisingly little kick. It just bounced in my hand. His buddies jumped back, I'm sure in reflex while Brandon jerked when the bullet hit him. A spray of blood came out his back. I remember there was a strong wind blowing in my face. I was close enough it carried his blood back to me in a fine mist. I had it on my arms and in my face, though it wasn't in large streaks. Just a fine, bright red spray. Little micro drops.

I had on a white shirt and it turned pink in places.

"Brandon was still standing, so I shot him again. This time in the head. I remember thinking the gun wasn't as deafening the second time as it was the first, but my ears were still ringing so I'm guessing my hearing was just stunned. This time, Brandon dropped like a stone. I'm short and he was tall, so the back and top of his head was just gone. Blood was everywhere.

"His friends scattered. No one tried to disarm me or talk to me. One of them had a cell phone and managed to call the cops. I just stood there. I had no intention of leaving. At that point, I honestly thought about taking my own life. I'm not sure why I didn't." She looked down at her hands then and shrugged. "I guess I just wasn't ready to die. At least, I didn't want my death to be linked with Brandon's."

"So you were fifteen when you killed him and went to trial. I take it they didn't even entertain the thought of trying you as a juvenile."

"No. And I didn't really care. I'd brought justice to that bastard and I owned that shit. I confessed immediately. The prosecutor in the case didn't want there to be any reason to overturn my confession so he made the judge assign me an attorney immediately. The guy did just enough to make it look like I had an adequate defense. He got the DA to agree to a plea of manslaughter. I got fifteen years. Would have been eligible for parole in four years."

"What happened?" I wasn't sure I wanted to hear any more, but if she could tell it, I could listen to it. After all, I'd asked her for this. In my mind, I was already plotting revenge on anyone who'd fucked her over, starting with her father and the judge who'd obviously pulled strings everywhere to save his son.

"The second I went to prison, I got hit hard by

the gangs. Pressuring me to work for them. The guards, too. They wanted me to help them get drugs to the prisoners and to… service them. I couldn't do much about the latter, but I never participated. In anything. When the gangs tried to beat me into submission, I took it. When the guards took what they wanted, I didn't fight them either. I did my best to make it not worth anyone's time to come at me. I wasn't fun to rape. I couldn't be relied on to deliver any product the gangs wanted to move. No matter what happened, I didn't fight back. In any way. I think, subconsciously, I was punishing myself by taking the beatings. It was horrible and I won't lie. I considered taking my own life again. I just didn't feel like I'd paid enough penance so I continued on. Just… taking whatever they dished out.

"It took about a year, but they all finally left me alone. Looking back, I think some of the guards were trying to get something on me to tack on to my sentence. That was probably the plan all along. I took a plea with the possibility I could get out in four years, but if I messed up and got extra time added on to my sentence, it pushed back my parole date."

"Did you get extra time?"

She shook her head. "No. But, like I said, I never expressed remorse for my crime. Every time, I said the same thing. The son of a bitch deserved it. Finally, after ten years, the parole board changed or something. The woman who conducted the hearing recounted every single interview I'd had over the years with psychiatrists, their own board, and anyone in an official capacity who'd ever asked me about my crime. She noted I always gave specific reasons for killing Brandon, noted that his trial was riddled with questions that would never be answered, and made a vehement argument that I'd served enough time. I wasn't a danger to anyone, I'd served way more than the minimum, and that I'd never been in trouble during my time in prison, even when I'd been bombarded with every disadvantage I could have had. She convinced the board to grant my parole and allow me to return to society. It was the first time since everything started that someone had taken my side and the impact nearly caused me to have a breakdown right there in front of the board."

Cotton took a deep breath. Before my eyes, her shoulders straightened and color filled her face. I hadn't realized how pale she'd been until that very moment. She seemed almost lighter. Like she'd just unburdened herself just by telling me, not only her version of events, but how she'd felt through each event.

"How did you end up here? In Somerset? Do you have family here?"

She shook her head. "No. I just wanted a place where I could disappear. Be left alone. The conditions of my parole said I had to stay in Kentucky, so I had them set me up with the parole office here. They gave me enough money for a room for a month and got me into that motel. They supposedly had a job ready for me, but when I showed up the owner said he didn't realize I'd been in for murder. And, no, he wasn't interested in the distinction between manslaughter and murder."

"Probably told the owner some shit to change his mind about hiring you, *and* put you in the path of illegal activities so you'd have a parole violation and get sent back."

"That's what I thought, too," she agreed softly.

"Cotton," I said, waiting until she met my gaze.

"You're safe here. Yeah, we're an MC, but we have close ties with the community and have more than a little pull with local police. Cain's reach is long and enduring. We're not always on the right side of the law, but he knows enough dirty shit on the right people to keep anything we do from coming to light. And we're *very* careful. The club has your back. More importantly, I have your back. We'll keep you safe, and there is no fuckin' way I'll ever let you go back to prison."

* * *

Cotton

Chase held my gaze for a long time after that. I could see him practically willing me to believe him. To trust him. I'm not sure I'd trusted anyone since the day Mary had been killed. It seemed like the whole world had been against me. Like I'd never be free to live my life. My childhood had been abruptly cut off and I'd started fighting for justice for my sister, then for the health and sanity of my parents. Then just to survive.

I nodded at Chase, realizing that, for the first time in a very long time, I actually believed someone when they told me they had my back. "I can't go back to prison. I've done everything I'm supposed to do since I landed in prison *and* got my parole. I've stayed out of trouble. I've kept my head down. I got a job."

"You did, sweetheart. And you found Bones. You found me."

"Why do you even care? For that matter, why would Cain risk his club? I'm not worth --"

"You're absolutely worth the risk, Cotton! Don't ever suggest otherwise."

To my complete and utter surprise, Chase reached for me, pulling me into his lap where we sat on the couch. I gave a surprised cry, but stilled when he wrapped me up in strong arms. He didn't restrain me, just held me comfortably. I was so shocked, I didn't struggle. It wasn't the invasion of my personal space as it was the sensation. A hug.

"How long has it been since I've been hugged?" I hadn't meant to say that out loud.

"Too long, apparently," Chase rumbled. I could feel his voice vibrating through his chest. Hesitantly, I rested my head on his chest next to his shoulder. His tantalizing scent had surrounded me in our close proximity, but now, with me cradled against his chest, his strong arms around me, I was overwhelmed by him. The scent was a combination of woodsy musk, gasoline fumes, and good clean sweat.

I tilted my head slightly, putting my nose in his neck. My lips parted and I heard myself whimper. Immediately, sweat erupted over my skin and my body trembled in his arms.

"Don't be afraid of me, Cotton." His hoarse plea made me cling to him. I fisted my fingers in his shirt realizing in that moment, I desperately wanted Chase to be mine.

"In my experience, men never take an interest in me unless they mean to hurt me." I looked up at him, needing to see his face, his eyes, when I asked my next question. "Do you want to hurt me, too?"

"Never!" His fierce whisper was vehement. The intensity in his eyes blazing down at me convinced me to believe him. If he'd wanted to hurt me, to take something I didn't freely give, he'd have done it already.

I sighed contentedly. "I'm going to choose to believe you, Chase. I'm going to believe and trust you." I looked up at him. "Please don't hurt me."

"Honey, no one in this whole Goddamned world will *ever* hurt you again. You get me? I'm claiming you in front of my club. Makin' you my ol' lady. In my world we'll be as good as married. I know it's sudden. You don't know me. I don't know you. But you'll not only have my protection, but the full protection of my club and our sister club if it becomes necessary. It also means that, if something happens to me, you'll have their continued protection. This is your home now, Cotton." He straightened his shoulders, puffing out his chest. "I'm your man."

I swallowed, nodding my assent. "Yes, Chase." I breathed the words like a prayer.

Very slowly, Chase lowered his head to mine. My breathing quickened, my heart rate shot up. I wanted his kiss. For the first time in my life, I fucking wanted this kiss more than I wanted to breathe.

"Please," I whimpered.

"Yes." Chase gave me what I wanted. His lips touched mine and I thought my whole body would go up in flames. This was bliss. Paradise. He was gentle, never taking when he could coax.

When I relaxed completely against him, Chase lapped at my lips, urging me to part them to receive more of his kiss. I did without hesitation, soaking up the affection like a drug. Chase threaded his fingers through my hair, holding me steady and angling my head exactly where he wanted it. I welcomed the instruction. I wanted to know how to please him as much as he was pleasuring me. Just from his kiss!

"Chase," I breathed against his lips. "Chase!"

"I know, honey. I've got you." He reassured me between kisses and sensual flicks of his tongue. "I've got you."

Long before I was ready, Chase lifted his head

and pulled me back against him. He was so strong. I felt so safe in his arms. It was like a safe cocoon I never wanted to leave. Gently, he rocked me side to side, soothing me when I was so ragged and raw. I felt like I'd been battered on the inside. Enclosed in the warmth of his arms, I grew drowsy. Then, for the first time since way before I went to prison, I fell asleep in a strange place surrounded by strange people...

And slept like the fucking dead.

Chapter Five

Cotton

I awoke practically naked and in a strange bed, wrapped in a layer of warmth. I wasn't in my cell. The bed was too comfortable for that. The smell not right at all. I inhaled deeply and moaned contentedly. Where I was at didn't matter. I'd never been so comfortable in my life.

Then a man nuzzled my neck. At first, I stiffened. Then his lips kissed from my ear to my shoulder and back in slow, velvety soft caresses and I relaxed once again.

"Where am I?" I sounded sleepy but as content as I felt.

"You're with me. In my bed." The male surrounding me with his warm body settled me tighter against him, my back to his front. Between us, snuggled into my backside, his cock gave an interested jerk.

"Chase?"

"Well, yeah, baby. Who else?"

"No one, I hope." I couldn't help but smile.

"Mmm," he grunted, settling back down.

"You sound as content as I feel. Do you often wake up with women in your bed?"

"Woman," he said. "Not plural. And no. You're the first."

I looked back at him. "You don't really expect me to believe that, do you?"

"Not sayin' I ain't fucked my share of women, Cotton. But I don't keep them in my bed, or even in my rooms. This is a first for me. One I intend to repeat with you every fuckin' night for the rest of my life."

"You don't know me, you know. What if I snore?

Or kick? What if you hate being around me?"

I felt him shrug, then squeezed me tighter. God, I loved this feeling! "You do snore, but I don't mind. You only kicked once. And if I hate being around you, I'll distract you with sex until your attitude changes. If that doesn't work, I'll paddle your ass."

"Wouldn't it be easier to just find someone you know? Someone you like?"

"What makes you think I don't know or like you?"

I had to think about that one. He knew more *about* me than any other person on the planet. He might not *know* me, but just the fact that he hadn't run away screaming from me told me a lot. Told me a lot about Cain and Pops, too.

"I don't lie, Chase, and I'm not starting now. I've latched on to you. Probably from the first moment I saw you. Larger than life. Laughing with your buddies in the bar. You represent every single thing I want in this life."

"You think so? What would that be, honey?"

"A home. Safety. A family. A man who… cares." I trailed off on the last because that's not what I wanted. Caring was nice, but I wanted the fairytale.

"Give me time, Cotton. I'll make a believer out of you. I'll make you never regret giving me a chance. I'll also make you fall in love with me so deeply you'll never want to leave."

My breath caught. I could feel my heart speeding up. "Don't say that, Chase. If I fall in love with you and you leave me…"

He moved to lean over me, urging me to my back while he settled himself on top of me. "I know you don't understand yet. You will, baby. I told you that makin' you my ol' lady was same as being married in my world. Understand me when I tell you takin' a woman as an ol' lady isn't done lightly. It's forever. We work shit out if we have problems. No divorce. I won't lie to you. I won't betray you. You'll be kept in the dark about club business for your own protection, but I will tell you anything you want to know. Because we're partners."

"You're confusing me, Chase. Let me up." I pushed at him but he just leaned down and kissed me gently.

"I'm moving way too fast for you. I know that. I'm movin' kinda fast for my own damned self, but it's done, baby. I've got your vest ordered. Texted Cheetah last night to start workin' on it."

"If you feel like you're moving too fast, why do it? You said no divorce. Shouldn't you wait until we're sure about each other?"

Chase was quiet for a long while, like he was mulling it all over. When he spoke, it was with conviction. "I never thought I'd put down roots. My own family was shit so I never really cared if I had one. Until Bones let me in. Sure, I could have all the pussy I wanted, but there was a difference in the men who had ol' ladies. They play hard. Enjoy their sensuality any way they want. But there is a respect for each other and... devotion? to one another I knew I wanted. But I never met a woman I wanted that with. Until I saw you."

"You said you don't cheat." I wanted this very clear. "I only want to make sure because you could easily break my heart, Chase. I was fifteen when I went away. I'm twenty-five now, but I might as well still be a child in the outside world. Relationships. Intimacy. I haven't been touched except to be hurt since before my sister died. Something as complicated as this? You and me? Here?" I shook my head. "I'm gone for you, Chase. I think you know that, too."

He stroked an errant curl off my forehead. I loved the feel of his weight on top of me and arched into him when he moved, whimpering when he put even a small amount of space between us.

"I thought you didn't know much about relationships."

"I don't. But I had to learn to read people well or I'd never have survived. You're... catnip. To me." I knew I wasn't making sense. But I had no idea how to explain my feelings.

He grinned. "I think I got you. At the bar, was I the first man in your adult life to protect you?"

I nodded. "But I was infatuated with you even before then. Because of how you treated everyone. You're a protector." When he raised an eyebrow, I rolled my eyes. "OK. That *and* you're sexy as hell."

Chase chuckled, lowering his head to kiss me once again. "Did you not hear the part where I was an assassin? Honey, I ain't a nice guy."

"Are you trying to talk me into this or out of it?"

"That's a nice look on you, you know." His grin was devastating as he smiled down at me.

"What is?"

With the pad of one fingertip, Chase traced my lips. "Your smile."

And yeah. My smile widened. My heart swelled. And I. Was. Done.

* * *

Chase

I was a bastard for playing on Cotton's emotions like this. But, Goddamnit, I wanted her to cling to me with all her might. I wanted her heart involved because mine damned sure was. Love at first sight always seemed the height of hilarity, but I'd damned sure been fallen for her the moment I laid eyes on her.

"I can't take you this morning, baby. Not if I want to have some self-respect later." Her brows knit together and she looked like I'd struck her. "Shh…" I kissed her again, lingering this time. The more I lingered, the less resolved I became. When I finally pulled away her eyes were glazed with pleasure. She clung to me sweetly and whimpered for more. "Let me finish. Believe me, I want you so fuckin' bad I ache with it." Emphasizing, I ground my cock against her mound. The only thing separating us was her underwear and my sleep shorts. "The very last thing in this world I want to do is take advantage of your state of mind. You want me, but you have a touch of hero worship. I just don't want you to regret it when it happens. I want you to embrace it. Embrace us. Because I'm gonna get to know you, you're gonna get to know me, and we're gonna be so in love with each other it fuckin' hurts, baby."

"You're not taking advantage of me, Chase." She shook her head for emphasis. "I've been locked up for ten years. *Ten years*. There were very few decisions I got to make. I'm not a virgin, but any sexual experience I've had hasn't been positive."

"Baby… fuck! You're killin' me!"

"Every single kiss you've given me, every single sweep of your tongue, has shown me what you're offering. Please don't make me wait one more second for it."

Yeah. I didn't have it in me to resist her sincere pleas. "I'm goin' to hell for this."

Cotton threaded her fingers through my hair and looked me in the eyes. "Then I'll join you there."

God, she was greedy! Once she got comfortable with kissing me and figured out what she liked, she was all about kissing. Lord, help me she was all about kissing. And she tasted like heaven. Rather than try to guide her, I just let her go. If it drove me slightly crazy, so much the better. Whatever it took for her to be comfortable with this.

Once she settled into kissing me, Cotton grew bolder in her exploration. Her hands roamed over my shoulder and bunched in my shirt. I could tell she wanted to pull it off, but was hesitant.

"Tell me," I said against her mouth. "Tell me what you want, baby."

"I..." She shuddered against me, flicking her tongue out to stroke mine. "I want us to get naked." As she confessed her need, she trembled in my arms. She didn't seem to mind me on top of her, pinning her down, but I tried my damnedest not to be aggressive, not to spook her. So help me God, this would be the best experience of her life. No matter what I had to do to make it so.

"Then pull my shirt off, baby. This is your time. Take what you want."

"But I want you to enjoy this too."

I couldn't help but chuckle. "There is no way for me not to have fun unless you don't have fun. So you do what you want to do. Explore. Ask questions. You can't do anything wrong."

She whimpered and clawed at my shirt, pulling it over my head. Then she struggled, trying to get her own shirt off. She seemed frustrated that she still had her bra on, but when I'd put her to bed last night I wasn't going into forbidden territory. I helped her and, once she was naked from the waist up, she pulled me against her flesh to flesh. I wanted to laugh with delight at her enthusiasm but the sensations were so sharp it was all I could do to keep up with her.

As if her instinct had taken over, she rubbed her breasts against my chest, groaning as she did. Her eyes were closed, a look of bliss on her lovely face. Her hips bucked, rubbing against my cock through her underwear and my shorts. The second she hit the right spot, her eyes flashed open and her legs tightened around my waist. With a cry, she worked herself over my cock, her breathing coming faster and faster until she shrieked, arching her back and neck as she came against me.

I braced myself on one arm, leaning down to kiss and suck her exposed neck, doing my best to prolong her pleasure and build more. The heat from her pussy made my dick pulse with need. Christ, I could feel her damp warmth almost like my cock was sliding through her lips to rub her clit like she needed!

It took her long, long moments, but soon her body relaxed and she stilled beneath me. I came to rest on top of her fully when she slid her slim arms round my neck and tugged me closer to her. Not to kiss me or for me to do anything, she just pulled me to her, rubbing her face against mine like a contented kitten. I slid my arms underneath her, wrapping them around her slender body, kissing her cheek and neck while she came down from her orgasmic high.

"I gotcha, baby," I said, smoothing her hair away from her face as I kissed her cheek. "I gotcha."

"Chase." Cotton's sigh was magical. There was so much wonder and excitement in that one word I wanted to puff my chest out and yell, "I did that!" I continued to give her soft little kisses until she cupped my face in her tiny hands and looked up at me. That same sense of wonder in her voice was now reflected in her eyes. "I never knew..."

"Honey, me neither. Ain't never experienced anything like this with a woman."

"Will you..." She swallowed and looked away. I gave her time to get herself together, not wanting to overwhelm her more than she already was. "Will you fuck me now?"

"No, Cotton. But I *will* make love to you."

At first, she'd looked like I'd torn out her heart, but when she realized I was going to give her what she wanted, she gave me an eager smile once again. I'd never particularly enjoyed taking an inexperienced woman. I expected her to know her way around a man's body, or at the very least, look out for her own pleasure. Not so with Cotton. I wanted to discover on my own what made her scream, sigh, whimper, and lose her Goddamn mind.

I sat up, pulling her panties from her hips and down her shapely thighs. Once free, she spread her legs automatically, letting them fall over my thighs once I'd pulled my pants down over my hips. I wanted to take my time, to worship her body like she deserved, but that would have to wait until the next time. This time, I was going to give her what she wanted. Then I'd show her how much better it could be.

I snagged a condom from the nightstand, tore it open and rolled it on. Cotton stared up at me wide-eyed, her breaths coming in short pants. "Talk to me, Cotton. You good or do we need to stop and catch our breath?"

"What? No! Are you kidding me?" She reached for me, pulling me to her. "Don't stop!"

My chuckle was smothered by her kiss, which I welcomed, humming as I deepened it, wanting to sweep her up in a sensual tide that took her over. Continuing to kiss her, I slid my cock to her entrance.

When the head penetrated her, I froze. She was so fuckin' tight! How the hell was I gonna last like this? Cotton looked up at me, her eyes wide, her lips parted in an "O" of surprise. She seemed frozen, not moving, not even breathing. Then her legs slowly tightened around my hips and she... shifted. Cotton tilted her pelvis, sliding her pussy along my length as she arched up, pushing onto me. She sucked in a breath before moving back, then forward again. All Cotton. I never moved an inch. If I had, I'd probably have come in an instant.

I waited until she stilled, her eyes wide with wonder before I started moving again. "You good, baby?" When she only nodded several times, I shook my head. "I need words, Cotton. I need to know you're OK."

"Yes," she said, nodding her head furiously, that smile once again gracing her lips. "I'm fabulous!"

"That's what I wanted to hear."

When I started a slow, steady rhythm, my body mashed against hers, my arms on the mattress beside her head, sweat broke out over my skin. There was no fucking way this was lasting long.

"Oh, wow," she whispered.

"Indeed."

Once I could tell she'd settled in to the sensations, I shifted my body so that I braced myself on one forearm while freeing the other to feather my thumb over her nipple. I urged her leg higher over my hip to get that friction on her clit I knew she needed. When my fingers closed around one nipple, she cried out, arching into my touch.

"Chase! Ah, God!"

Cotton moved her pelvis, speeding up my slow and steady pace. I didn't really want to go faster. I was in danger of ending this all too fucking soon, but what Cotton wanted this time, Cotton got.

It wasn't long before she was crying out in little grunts and gasps as I drove into her. When her cunt spasmed around my cock and she let go an ear-splitting scream, I joined her into oblivion.

Like a geyser, I exploded, the latex the only barrier between us. It was necessary, but I cursed it. I wanted Cotton to me mine in every fucking way possible. If she got pregnant, so much the better. She'd stay with me because she had no other choice. But I'd done the right thing and protected her.

Right. Like I wasn't regretting that now.

It took long moments before I was able to catch my breath. Cotton still looked up at me with that adorable bemused expression on her face.

"Did that just happen?" Her question was asked softly, her smile growing wider. That expression like she thought I hung the moon growing with each passing second.

"Yeah, baby. That happened." I groaned and rolled off her, taking her with me. "Give me a second and I'll get us cleaned up."

"Wow," she said.

"Yeah. Good word for it."

"No other way to describe that." She snuggled into my side, her thigh sliding up mine possessively as she clung to my shoulder.

"Do you hurt? You're incredibly tight."

"It burns a little, but in a good way."

"Want a soak in the tub? Might ease any discomfort."

She looked up at me, suddenly unsure. "I

don't..."

"Room enough for both of us if you don't mind me with you." When her expression relaxed, I knew I'd said the right thing. She was insecure about her place with me and what she was allowed to do or ask. That had to change, but it was completely up to me to make sure she was comfortable enough with me to tell me what she wanted.

"Good. Just give me a minute. You wore me out."

Her laughter was delighted and maybe just a touch relieved. "You did me, too."

"Gonna have to build my stamina if I'm gonna keep up with my younger woman. I'm an old man."

"You can't be more than thirty-five or so," she said, raising up to look at me. "That's definitely not old."

"Thirty-eight," I said. "And it's not. But you're still the young chick craving sex." I rolled over, burying my face in her neck and shaking my head, letting my beard tickle her. She shrieked and squirmed, trying to get away, but continuing to laugh. "That's what I thought. Come on. Let me get rid of this fuckin' condom then we'll soak for a while."

"Thank you, Chase." Looking at Cotton smile would never get old. "That was the most wonderful thing I've ever experienced."

"You never have to thank me for loving you, honey. It was the most wonderful experience I've ever had, too." I kissed her gently, then we went to the bathroom to clean up.

Chapter Six

Cotton

The next few weeks were filled with so many activities it made my head swim. My favorites included swimming, movies, and, oddly, cooking. But, by far, my most favorite thing of all was riding Chase's bike. OK, so I didn't ride it by myself. I rode behind Chase while he took me all over the state. We took the interstates and bigger roads and it was like flying!

Always, he had at least four of his brothers with us. I'd learned that was how they thought of the members of their club. They were brothers and sisters. Even the ol' ladies were called their sisters. It wasn't just a name either. They treated each other like I imagined a close, loving family would treat each other. Chase was right. I'd found my home.

Also, Chase and Carnage had decided I needed to learn how to drive. While in my previous life it had been something I'd been eager to attain, now I was more than a little nervous. I soon got the hang of it, though. Before I knew it, I'd been driving all over the Bones compound running errands inside the property for anyone who needed something. I was having the time of my life. I felt like a kid, taking every opportunity I could to drive and pretending I was out on the open road, looking forward to the time I could actually leave home and go anywhere in the city I wanted to. Even though Chase wanted me to take some more time to practice before I took my actual driving test, I occasionally snuck out on my own. Just to experience driving on the open road by myself.

The first time I'd done it, Chase had actually spanked me. Which I'd enjoyed more than he'd intended. That had led to some explosive sex, which he told me would never happen again. I'd smirked, knowing that wasn't something he could deny either of us no matter how stern he looked. The club mechanic, Tool, had given me a little lime green Fiesta. It was the one Chase had insisted I learn on because, as he put it, it was safe, but was something no one would miss if it disappeared. I got the feeling a lime green Fiesta wasn't the sort of car an MC wanted parked in front of the clubhouse. As evidenced by the fact they'd kept it in the very back corner of the garage. With a tarp over it. With a sign that said, "Do Not Remove Tarp."

Now, it was parked outside by the back of the garage under the same tarp. With the same sign only this time the tarp was held down with cement blocks so the wind didn't blow it off. I often drove it around so no one stopped me when I removed the tarp, got in and took off. Slowly.

I drove around the property for a little while with the windows rolled down. I waved at the few people I saw along the way. Everyone smiled and waved back, some calling out a greeting.

I knew I'd get in trouble, but when I saw no one was at the gate to the compound, I grinned and rolled through. The road to the club property was just a little one lane road, nestled in the hills around Pulaski County. Rarely was anyone on the road except motorcycles and usually only in the evenings as people filed into the Boneyard. Even the bar was a couple miles from the compound so I had the road mostly to myself.

It wasn't until I rounded the first sharp curve that I realized I was in trouble. I let off the gas and pushed the brake to slow before reaching the bend and, though the car slowed somewhat, it didn't slow nearly enough. The pedal went all the way to the floor with very little resistance. It was only then I noticed a light on that had never lit up before.

I almost made the turn, but there was a small limb in the road. Normally, I'd just roll over it, but in my panic, I jerked the wheel and the car spun. I screamed as the vehicle made a complete turn before dropping off into a ditch and slamming into the rock wall beside it. My heart pounded as I sat there taking stock of the aftermath. The car hit on the driver's side, but, thankfully, in the back. While my door was pinned and I was roughed up a bit, I didn't take the brunt of the impact.

For long moments, I sat there, my hands on the wheel, not moving. Just trying to breathe. I was in so much trouble… The very last thing I wanted to do was call Chase. While I kind of enjoyed the spanking before, this was different. Nothing had happened to me or the car the club had so generously let me borrow the first time. Now, however. Yeah. It wasn't the spanking I dreaded, but the look of disappointment on Chase's face.

And what if the cops got here first? I had no idea if driving without a license violated my parole, but it couldn't help my situation. Why hadn't I thought of that before? Oh, God! I was in so much trouble!

Adrenaline kicked in and I climbed over the console to the passenger seat but couldn't get the door open. The ditch was deep, the door pinned by the lip of the trench. I put the car in battery mode so I could roll down the window and climb out, barely remembering to grab the phone Chase had given me before I started running back down the road toward the clubhouse. Until I heard the roar of a motorcycle coming from that direction.

My first instinct was to hide. But if it was Chase

coming after me, he'd be even more pissed if he had to hunt for me. Besides, I knew he'd worry if he came on that wreck -- or one of his brothers did and called him -- and I was nowhere to be found. So I stopped and waited. Sure enough, Chase and Deadeye came roaring up the road with two prospects trailing them. I thought it was Cliff and Daniel, but I couldn't be sure.

I just stood there until Chase and Daniel pulled up beside me. Deadeye and Cliff kept on going to the car and immediately started assessing the damage.

Chase shut down his bike and stalked around it to me. At least that's what it felt like. I took a step backwards before I found my spine and planted my feet. I fucked up. I'd accept the consequences.

"I'm sorry," I said softly. "I'll pay for the damage to the car."

Chase looked like I'd slapped him. "Could give a Goddamned fuck about the fuckin' car, woman! Are you hurt?" He pulled me into his arms and held me tightly. I could feel his big body shuddering around me like he was terrified. This big, gruff biker. The man who had admitted to being an assassin. There's no way I was reading this situation correctly. He was probably pissed as hell I'd disobeyed him. It had been a stupid move on my part, one I was prepared to pay for.

"I'm so sorry," I said again, doing my best to keep the tears at bay. I'd take my punishment like an adult.

"Cotton." He pulled back, holding me by my shoulders and forcing me to look up at him. "Are you. All. Right."

I blinked up at him, confused. "I--I'm fine. But the car --"

"Is a piece of shit. It's what we give everyone when they're learning to drive. We expect it to get beat up. It's easy to fix and to keep safe. That's why we keep it around."

"You told me not to leave before and I ignored you. I'm not supposed to be driving outside the compound."

"No, you're not. But every kid learning to drive does the exact same thing. More than one of them has wrecked in this exact same spot. Only, from the looks of things, you didn't hit the brakes. Took the curve too fast and lost control."

"That's pretty much it, except I *did* hit the brakes. The car slowed, but not much and not quickly enough. I pushed 'em hard, too. Usually when I hit them that hard, the car jerks to a stop, but it didn't do that this time. It's never done that."

"We'll figure it out." He pulled me back into his arms. "Are you sure you're OK, baby?"

"Yeah. Just shaken up. And worried you're mad at me."

"Oh, make no mistake. I'm gonna heat your ass for this. You took ten years off my life!"

"How did you even know I'd wrecked?"

"Remember I said it's what everyone here uses when they're learning to drive? Well, we've got a safety system in the car. It lets Data track where it is and if something happens. When you crashed, it sent him an alert. We came after you immediately."

"I'm so sorry, Chase."

"It's OK. Honest. Still spankin' your ass."

I couldn't help it. Even given the circumstances, I might have giggled. Just a little.

"I know that sound." Chase's voice was a rumbling growl in my ear. His chest vibrated with the gruff sound. It was equal parts aggression and lust. "Someone isn't intimidated by my threats. I think she might be turned on."

"Told you I don't lie. So maybe I should just not say anything."

"That's what I thought." He threaded his fingers through my hair and tilted my head back to kiss me. As always, I lost myself in his kiss. I could taste fear and determination. Had I really worried him that much? If so, I needed to do something to make up for it.

"You two need a minute?" Daniel spoke with an abundance of amusement in his voice. "Because I can totally move on down the road back to the clubhouse."

Chase growled and gave a heavy sigh as he ended the kiss and held his forehead to mine. "Fuck." He wrapped his arms tighter around me and just held me for long moments before responding to Daniel. "Fuck off, asshole. We're coming."

The light chuckle from the other man said he didn't take offense. "Yeah. That's what I was afraid of."

Chase glared at Daniel before tossing me a helmet and climbing on his bike. He didn't have to tell me to get on behind him. Once I was settled, we sped off down the road, Daniel just ahead of us.

As we entered the gate, a big Ford with a trailer headed out. The man in the truck waved as we passed, a big grin on his face. Chase pulled up to the garage before shutting down his bike. I got off and handed the helmet to him as he dismounted himself. Once it was lashed down, he pulled me back into his arms again.

"Scared me, girl," he said roughly.

"I'm sorry. I won't ever do it again." He barked out a laugh.

"If I had a nickel for each time I'd heard that." Tool came out of the garage, cleaning a wrench with a dirty rag. The man had a big grin on his face. "I take it you're good, Cotton?"

"Yeah. I'm fine. I'm sorry about the car."

Tool waved that off. "Did she do enough damage I can finally bury that piece of shit car?" Not only did Tool not look put out, he actually looked hopeful.

"Not sure, but my gut says no. She just banged the back end a bit. Check the brakes, though. She says they went to the floor."

That got a frown from Tool. "You sure, Cotton? All the way to the floor?"

"I think. I mean, I went easy, but the car didn't slow much. Just stopped accelerating where I'd taken my foot off the gas. When it didn't slow much, I panicked and hit them hard and it still didn't slow. Well, not enough anyway."

"Maybe you just lost control when you hit them too hard," Tool speculated, then shrugged. "We'll see. If there's something wrong with the brakes, I need to have my ass kicked. I always make sure to do a thorough check on that car because only inexperienced drivers use it since Cain got Angel that Mustang."

I heard a diesel engine rattling and turned to see the truck rolling through the gate with the little Fiesta. Poor thing looked sad and tired. Like it had been beaten up one too many times. Great. Now I was feeling sorry for a fucking car.

"We'll find out what happened," Tool said. "And…" He sighed heavily. "Unless there's something majorly wrong, it looks like little Feisty there will live to roll another day."

Chase grabbed my hand and tugged. "Come on, baby. Let's get outta here."

"I'm sorry for the extra work, Tool."

"Sweetheart, last time someone brought that car back from a wreck, I had to rebuild the front end. This ain't nothin', little lady. Don't worry your pretty head about it. I'll have it ready for you in a day or two."

"Thanks, Tool. But I think I've had my fill of driving for a while."

Chase dragged me away then took me upstairs to our room. Once inside, he locked the door before turning around to face me. When he did, the look in his eyes made me take a step backward.

"Are you gonna cut me loose?" The words nearly stuck in my throat. I had no idea how I'd recover if Chase decided I was just too much trouble to fool with.

If possible, he only grew more furious. "If you think you're gettin' outta this because of one stupid accident, you can think again. Now you get your ass over here and let me look you over."

I felt like a deer being stalked. The fine hair on the back of my neck stood up, warning me there was more going on inside Chase than he wanted to admit. Or maybe than I was ready for. But one thing I knew for certain was he'd never harm me. Sure, he'd spank my ass if he thought it was needed, but he'd never truly harm me. And any spanking he'd give me would end up with indescribable pleasure.

"I'm sorry, Chase." I stepped forward, stopping in front of him. He was tall and I had to crane my neck to look up into his face.

He grabbed the back of my neck, pulling me close to him so he could hold me still for his kiss. Heat seemed to smolder between us, the need to claim and possess, to take comfort from his body after my fright. A desperation I couldn't deny. Chase seemed to need the same thing I did because he started tugging and yanking at my clothing until I was standing before him in my underwear.

"Take it off, Cotton," he growled. "Take it off or

I'm takin' it off for you."

Hastily, I moved to comply with his orders. "You get naked, too," I said. "If I'm naked, you're naked."

He bared his teeth at me, obviously taking offense at my command but doing it anyway. The second he stripped the last item of clothing from his body, Chase was on me. He pulled me against him, wrapped his arms around me, and kissed me like there was no tomorrow. It was dominant and rough. Almost violent. His tongue thrust deep and he nipped at my bottom lip.

Squatting slightly, Chase lifted me, his arm under my ass. My legs went around his waist automatically and he wasted no time in cramming his cock inside me. I cried out, the fullness an invasion I hadn't been ready for. When he swatted my ass, I gave a sharp yelp.

"Still," he bit out. "Keep your legs around my waist and don't you fuckin' move."

He sounded angry, but his cock throbbed inside me with the beat of his heart. My pussy clenched down around him. He was long and thick and each time he fucked me I still had to adjust. This time he gave me no quarter. I took all of him, my body eager even as the burn bordered on pain.

Chase took us to the bed where he planted a knee and brought us both down on the mattress. His body weight pinned me down, not letting me move beneath him.

"There was a bruise on your hip," he accused.

"Seatbelt." The word came out a little high pitched, almost a squeak.

"At least you did that. Are you hurt, Cotton? And don't give me bullshit to try to make me calm down. I want the truth from you." The look in his eyes bordered on wild. He was at the limit of his control. He was as far inside me as he could get. Just holding himself there.

"Ah, God, Chase! Please move! I need you to fuck me." What was supposed to be a demand turned into a plea. I tried to move in him, but Chase smacked the outside of my thigh. Hard.

"Fuckin' answer the Goddamned question, Cotton!"

"No! I'm not hurt! Please Chase! Please!"

"You took ten fuckin' years off my life! Never do that again, do you hear me? Never! You could've been hurt. Then where would I be, huh? Where the Goddamned fuck would I be without you?"

With a savage grunt, Chase started to move, slamming into me hard. His hips pistoned back and forth, fucking me in brutal thrusts that skirted the edge between pain and pleasure. In a way, the slight pain was as much a turn on as anything else. Chase had never taken me so hard. He'd always been careful. Now, though, it was as if all the anger -- and fear? -- he had inside him manifested itself in this one display. He didn't hold back, just took what he needed. Gave what he could. But mostly, this was about him needing to assure himself I was, indeed, still here and to punish me for scaring him.

I held on for dear life, twining my arms around his neck. Chase's mouth was at my throat and he bit down hard, pinning me beneath him like an animal might do his mate. It didn't take long for both of us to come. I screamed my release as I tried to meet his thrusts with thrusts of my own. His weight prevented most of my movements, but I still tried. My nails clawed into the skin of his back as I rode out the incredible pleasure.

Then, with one final hard thrust, Chase threw back his head and roared his own orgasm. His back arched and the muscles in his neck, chest, and shoulders bulged. The veins and tendons in his neck stood out in stark relief. Never had I seen a more fantastic sight.

When he finally relaxed, he collapsed on top of me, his weight once more pinning me beneath him. I stroked the hair at the nape of his neck, petting him like I might a wild beast who'd decided to let me tame him briefly.

We lay like that for a long time, both of us breathing hard. Finally, Chase kissed the spot on my neck where he'd bitten, licking and nuzzling the small hurt in apology. "Did I hurt you too badly, honey?"

"You didn't hurt me at all. Anything you did gave me pleasure. Rough pleasure, but pleasure all the same."

"You sure? Don't lie to me."

"I swear I'm not lying, Chase. There were times when it was a bit uncomfortable, but it only added to the pleasure."

He sighed. "You scared the life out of me, baby. I can't lose you. Not now. Not ever."

"I'm so sorry." Tears threatened and I did my best to blink them back. "You've been nothing but good to me. Your whole club has. And I went and did the one thing you told me not to do."

Rolling us to our sides, Chase stroked a lock of hair away from my forehead out of my eyes. "Honey, I could care less if you go outside the compound. Every single person who's learned to drive here has done the exact same thing. I told you, more than one have wrecked in that exact same spot. Probably the exact same way you did. I'm not mad about that. Hell, I'm not mad at you for *anything*. When Data told me about the alert from the safety system on your car, I nearly lost my mind. I can't lose you, Cotton. Not for any reason." He took a breath, closing his eyes briefly. "I fuckin' love you, Cotton. More than anything in this whole Goddamned world."

I sucked in a breath. Tears formed I had no control over. Then I gave him a watery smile. "I love you too, Chase. I love you so much!"

We held each other tightly for long moments. Then Chase's cock twitched inside me, coming back to life. Which was when it hit me and I barked out a laugh.

"Guess it's a good thing you *do* love me."

"Why's that, baby?"

"We just had sex."

"Not sure you could classify that as mere sex. That was straight up fuckin'." He grinned. "Damned good fuckin'."

"Right. But that's not what I mean."

He looked puzzled. "Not followin'."

"You came inside me, Chase. Without a condom."

Chase just looked at me before his eyes widened slightly as understanding dawned on him. Then he grinned, pulling me on top of him so I straddled his hips. He kissed me, lingering until I was panting with need and his dick was twitching like mad inside my pussy.

"What are you doing?" Not that I really cared. If it got me more of that glorious pleasure he was so fond of dishing out, I'd do whatever he wanted me to do.

"Gettin' ready to fuck you again. Makin' sure it takes."

I gasped, trying to pull back so I could see his

face. "What? You can't be serious."

"Can't I?" He thrust his hips, driving his shaft deeper inside me before relaxing once again.

"Chase, I've got at least five years before I can even think about getting pregnant." But I didn't pull away from him. Instead, I rose and fell on his cock, finding a slow, lazy rhythm designed to draw out the coming pleasure.

His hands rubbed up and down my back. "Why's that, baby?"

"I'm still on probation. Any little slip up -- like the one today -- and there's a high probability I'll go back to prison." I shook my head, stopping my movements as the reality truly sank in. "I can't go back to prison if I'm pregnant. I'd never be able to stop myself from fighting back and, with the reputation I already had, they'd be merciless in attacking me. Just for the fun of it. No way I make it through a pregnancy without losing the baby." I tried to roll off Chase, but his arms clamped around me like a vise.

"You listen to me, Cotton, and you listen good." His whole demeanor changed. He'd started to lighten up a bit, but now he was back to being aggressive. "You ain't goin' back to prison. Not for any reason. There's even a hint that's comin' down and you and I will disappear. No one will ever find us. But under no circumstances are you goin' back to prison. I'll kill every motherfucker I have to to keep that from happening. You get me?"

I looked into his eyes. This was the first time I could actually see the kind of killer he was. I could finally reconcile the Chase Dutton I knew with the assassin he'd told me he'd been in a former life. That man was still there. Buried deep, but there nonetheless. "I understand," I whispered.

"Good. You see me, don't you." He knew I saw the ruthless killer inside him. Had probably let that side of him show on purpose to drive his point home. "This is the man you've given yourself to. The man who'll protect you and our children with deadly force. I'd give my life to protect you, honey, but only if I can't kill a motherfucker. There is no world where you or our children are not protected from everything and everyone who wants to harm you. That includes anyone trying to take you back to prison. It ain't happening, Cotton."

Again, I nodded. I should have been horrified. Scared even. Instead, I was elated. Joy burst through me in an unexpected fireworks display. Here was someone who truly loved me. Who was willing to kill to keep me safe.

"I don't deserve you, Chase," I said, my voice breaking. "But I'm not letting you go. I want you for my very own and I don't care if I deserve you or not!" I burst into tears.

I wrapped my arms tightly around Chase's neck, burying my face in his neck as I sobbed like a baby. Chase held me as tightly as I held him. He just let me cry, clinging to me as I clung to him.

When my tears finally slowed, Chase rolled us over, never lessening his hold on me. Then he started to move inside me. He kissed the side of my neck. My jaw. My face. When he settled on my lips, I opened for him eagerly, needing to kiss him more than anything. I tasted my tears on his tongue where he'd kissed them away. When he took us both to bliss, I cried out his name and reveled as his hot seed spilled inside me once again.

Chase gazed down at me as he stroked my hair, his cock still firmly embedded in my pussy. "You deserve a man better than me, Cotton. But I'll be ruthless in protecting you. I'll give you anything you want if it's within my power to provide it. And I'll love you until the end of my days."

He leaned down and kissed me gently before finally sliding out of me. He scooped me up and took me to the bathroom where he washed us both. After he'd cleaned me, I sat on the vanity, Chase standing between my spread legs, his forehead against mine.

"I love you, Cotton. Don't ever scare me like that again. Not sure my heart can take it."

"Just so you know, I'm done driving. I'll just go with you from now on."

He chuckled. "Nope. You're getting your license. Never know when you might need it and takin' care of you means makin' sure you can take care of yourself sometimes."

"Ugh," I grumbled, wrapping my arms around his neck and burying my face there. "Don't wanna."

"I know, baby. But when you get bucked off, you gotta get back on the horse."

"Maybe I could learn to ride a horse instead. It's bound to be easier. Fewer parts to worry about."

His chuckle warmed me and made me smile. "Sure. But it's hot in the summer and cold in the winter. Besides, we don't have a barn."

"Fine," I grumped. "I'll try again."

"That's my girl." He gave me a hard kiss before pulling back to look at me. "Now. About that spanking…"

Chapter Seven

Chase

"Where's Cotton?" I was surprised when Tool approached me, a frown on his face.

"She's moving into our new house in the neighborhood. What's up?" I didn't like the frown on the other man's face.

"She was right. The brakes went to the floor when she tried to stop. I owe that girl an apology. You too, brother." I'd never seen Tool look so out of sorts. He was pacing back and forth when I found him in the garage, muttering to himself. Fixing the Fiesta hadn't been top on the list of priorities, so it had been a couple days before anyone had gotten around to looking at it. Now, it seemed like there was definitely something more important that we'd first thought.

"Hum... is it finally time to retire that abomination of color?" I couldn't help the grin on my face. We all complained about it being too girly of a car to belong to an MC but Angel refused to let us get rid of it entirely. Since it was technically still her car, there wasn't much we could do. Cain always looked put out when someone mentioned getting rid of it, like he commiserated but I suspected it was a source of great amusement to him.

"No," Tool said, becoming more agitated. "This was *my* fault."

"What?" That surprised me. And took away any amusement I'd first felt. Accidents were one thing. Something preventable was a different bird altogether. "How is it your fault?"

"Thing didn't have no brake fluid. I'm surprised she didn't notice the light on the dashboard. Probably did and just didn't know what it was." He looked up at me with a stricken expression. "Chase, I'm sorry. I have no idea how I missed that. I always inspect all the fluid levels, but somehow, I just missed this. I even had the maintenance sticker on the car *and* my log book marked as having checked it."

My first instinct was to beat the man's face in, but Tool was nothing if not a thorough, highly competent mechanic. He and Carnage kept every single vehicle in the club in top notch working order. Even though it could have ended differently, I tried my best to stifle my anger.

"I'm sure it's not something that will ever happen again." I knew a muscle in my jaw ticked, but Tool didn't push back. The man was likely beating himself up more than I ever could.

"No, Chase. It won't." He sighed. "I'm gonna have Carnage bring every vehicle I serviced in the last few weeks, startin' with the ol' ladies. We're gonna go over everything together. Just to make sure."

I sighed, trying to rein it an and look at the situation logically. "It was an accident, Tool. No one's perfect."

"It's not an accident that should have happened. There are checklists for a reason. For some reason, I marked the brake fluid as being OK when I didn't do it." He scrubbed the back of his neck with his hand. "I don't know how I missed the brakes. Stupid ass mistake that could have gotten your girl killed. Or someone else."

"Yeah." I shook my head, taking a deep breath for control. "It could have." It was a dick thing to say, but I left Tool after that. I was about to lose my temper and I knew I'd regret it if I didn't at least think about it before I beat the fuck out of him. If there was one thing I'd learned from Cotton it was to not judge people based on one incident. I'd known Tool for years. The man was excellent at his job. If he hadn't been, Cain would never have given him the position as club mechanic. Everyone had off days. I still didn't like it. I was going to have to think about this one for a while.

It had been two days since Cotton's accident and I still wasn't over it. Though I tried to not think about it, every time I thought about her going out without me, I nearly had a panic attack. It wasn't that I didn't trust her or thought she wasn't capable of doing things by herself. Everyone had to learn how to fucking drive sometime in their life. With learning came mishaps, most of them minor. Like this one. It could have been way worse than it had turned out. No. It was that I hated not being there to protect her. To be fair, she didn't seem to want me out of her sight much either. I'd only left today because I felt like a pussy. She hadn't said anything, but I could tell she didn't like not going with me.

While I tried to rationalize my actions by telling myself she needed some time to herself so she didn't feel like she was smothered or trading one prison for another, I still hated every single second of it. So, instead of doing the other errands I had planned on doing, I found myself headed back to the little house we'd claimed within the club property.

Until the last couple of years, most everyone had lived in the big clubhouse. Any property everyone else had owned, or if someone wanted to live in a house outside the clubhouse, it had been outside the protection of the club. Bones wasn't that big and we enjoyed each other's company. But with the addition of so many kids and the growing families, Cain had decided it was time to expand the grounds. The club had over five hundred acres with the option to buy out a couple of our neighbors if we wanted to. So we'd fenced in the place and started building our own private neighborhood.

The houses were spaced out so there was plenty of privacy while still being within walking distance of anywhere within the compound. Our house was near the center of the current neighborhood. It was close enough for us to be near everyone, but far enough away I could make her scream my name during sex with the windows open and we wouldn't get too much attention.

Just the thought of how responsive Cotton was to me lifted my spirits a little. She had so many reasons to keep her distance, yet she'd given me a chance with her fragile heart. I vowed I'd always protect her, no matter the cost to myself. Which meant I'd need to go back and throw Tool a beating. But not now. I'd wait until I'd fucked Cotton again. Which would happen the second I walked in the door. I needed her body around mine so I could fuckin' think clearly, knowing she was good and unharmed. When I thought about what had happened too much, when I got so anxious I could barely breathe for worrying about her, fucking her until I lost my self in her body and gentle spirit was the only way I could pull myself together. If making love to her didn't mellow me out, I'd see how badly I needed to beat Tool before I felt better.

I arrived at home to the smell of something burning. I hurried to the kitchen and smoke was rolling from the oven door. Opening it only made it billow out in great black rolls.

"Cotton?" I yelled her name as I pulled out the pan filled with what had probably been cookies but now resembled burnt cow patties. "Cotton!"

I opened a window just as the smoke detector

started blaring. I swore as I tossed the pan and all out the back door before unhooking the screeching alarm.

"Cotton!" I was starting to get worried now. Sure, it was possible she'd forgotten the cookies in the oven and left, but I didn't think so. She was always hyper aware of what she was baking simply because she was always so excited to see how her creations turned out.

As I stepped down the hall, I glanced in the open bathroom door before I passed, and did a double take. Cotton lay on the floor, her head against the bathtub. Water was on the floor in front of the sink. Was there a leak coming from the cabinet under it? She was unconscious.

"Cotton! Cotton!" I roared her name, gripping her shoulders and shaking her slightly before pulling her into my arms. I felt for a pulse and nearly pissed myself in relief when I found one. I pulled out my cell and called the clubhouse.

"I need Mama and Pops," I said without preamble to whomever answered. "Cotton's hurt."

There was a curt reply, but I knew the older couple would be ready when I got Cotton there. I managed to get her in my truck and sped all the way to the clubhouse. I think I talked to her the entire way though I have no idea what I actually said. It was more to comfort myself, trying to convince myself she was going to be all right.

"Fuck, Cotton! Please! Fuckin' wake up! Put me out of my misery, baby."

I skidded the truck to a stop in front of the clubhouse. Three of my brothers rushed out to meet us. Pops had the passenger door open the second it was unlocked. He pulled Cotton into his arms and hurried into the house with her, me close on his heels.

"What happened?" Mama was all business as she started examining Cotton.

"She fell," I said, assuming that was what had happened. "Found her on the floor. Looked like she hit her head on the bathtub.

"And you moved her?" Mama's head snapped up, her gaze alarmed.

"Yes, I moved her! I had to get her here for help!"

"If she's broken her neck, Chase, she could be paralyzed. Or worse."

I hadn't thought of that. I felt like I'd been sucker punched and my knees gave way. I collapsed in a chair behind me, my whole world crashing down around me. "Fuck."

"Mama…" Pops said warningly.

"Well, he's military! He knows better!"

"When someone you love is involved, it's hard to think clearly. The boy's watching his heart laying there injured. Don't torture him."

Mama glared at Pops but refrained from staying anything else.

"Chase?" The small whimper came from Cotton. I nearly passed out in relief when she tried to sit up.

"Hush, now," Mama said. "Chase is right here. Give me a minute and you can see him."

"I'm here, baby," I said, trying to move closer to Cotton, but when I stood the room seemed to tilt and I fell back to the chair. Pops was there instantly, shoving my head between my knees.

"Take a breath, son. She's all right."

"She was movin', Pops."

"Yeah, she was. That's a good sign."

"I didn't hurt her." God, I sounded like such a pussy, but Goddamnit, I'd never forgive myself if I'd inadvertently made things worse.

"No, son. Just take a few deep breaths there. You gotta be strong for when Mama's done. Your girl'll need you."

Mama fussed over Cotton for at least an hour, taking X-rays and CT scans. Never had I been so glad Cain had insisted Mama have the best equipment possible as I was in that moment. What had seemed like overkill when I'd first come to Bones was now the sweetest salvation I'd ever known. Cain said it came in handy when the boys came back from a tour with ExFil if things went sideways, but I suspected now he did it for situations like this one. He wanted his people protected. Since Mama was a retired Army surgeon, she knew her shit when it came to this stuff. If she wanted it, Cain provided.

By the time she was finished, I'd gotten my wits about me and could stand without falling on my face. I took Cotton's hand and kissed her knuckles. "Hey, baby."

"I burnt the cookies, didn't I?"

"Honey, don't worry about the fuckin' cookies. You can make more if you want. I'm worried about you."

"I got hit in the head," she said, looking up at me, her eyes drooping in exhaustion.

"I know, honey. But I got you to Mama. She's makin' sure you're OK."

"Scans are all negative," Mama said from behind me. She moved to Cotton's other side and stroked the girl's hair gently. "Got a hell of a goose egg on her head, but she's fine. I can't figure how she hit her head so hard-on the bathtub but didn't hurt her neck. It's a miracle I'd say. And thank God for it."

Cotton frowned, looking confused. "But I didn't hit the bathtub."

"Honey, that's how I found you. On the floor with your head on the tub where you fell."

"But I got hit before I fell."

"There was water on the floor," I said, running my lips back and forth over the back of her hand. It seemed to comfort her as much as it comforted me. "Looked like you slipped and fell."

She shook her head slowly. "No... I'm pretty sure I got hit first." Then she furrowed her brows. "But how could that have happened? I remember getting hit, then... nothing."

"Don't worry about it now, dear. You need to rest. Not give yourself a worse headache by trying to remember too much. It will come. If not, don't worry about it. It's not unusual when you have a head injury to forget the events leading up to it and immediately after."

"Besides," Pops said. "How could you have possibly hit your head without falling? Did you bump it on a cabinet?"

"No. There's nothing in there to bump my head on."

"Maybe you were crawling under the sink to see where the water was coming from?" Pops asked the question, obviously trying to look at every possibility.

"No," I said. "I found her next to the tub. If she'd knocked herself out under the sink --"

"You'd have found her there," Pops finished for me. "Well, the only other thing to consider is if someone hit her, and that's impossible."

There was silence in the room while Mama put an ice pack on Cotton's head over the pumpknot. It wasn't impossible, but I wanted to think it was impossible. Because, if someone hit her, that meant an intruder was able to break into our compound, our homes. And that was the one scenario I absolutely would not entertain.

I wouldn't.

* * *

Cotton

It took several days, but the pumpknot on my head was finally going down. Chase hadn't let me out of his sight since the accident. The events leading up to it were still a bit fuzzy, but I was certain I hit my head *before* I fell. Not after. I also had a vague impression of being moved next to the bathtub, but that was even more muddy. Unfortunately, the harder I tried to remember, the more of a headache I got. And the muddier my memories got. I honestly couldn't tell they were actual memories or a sinister dream.

"Ready to go, baby?" Chase rested his hands on my shoulders where I sat at the vanity in our bedroom. I was finishing up my hair and what little bit of makeup I wore. He kissed the top of my head. He was taking me out tonight. I'd begged him to go back to the bar. I wanted to see my friends and some of the patrons. Other than Butch and his bunch, I'd have really enjoyed my time at the bar if I hadn't been so worried about keeping my nose clean. It was a fun, if rowdy, bunch most of the time.

I smiled up at him. "I'm ready. Thank you, Chase. Thanks for taking me on."

"Honey, I'm pretty sure it was you takin' me on. The rest of the guys keep tellin' me I don't deserve you and that someone will come along and convince you to throw your lot in with someone a lot younger and better looking."

As I'd hoped, that got a giggle out of her. "Never! You're my one and only."

"Now, that's what I like to hear." He leaned in and kissed my lips gently. "Let's go. Got a bunch of the brothers and their ol' ladies gonna be there. We'll have a ball."

"I can't wait." The excited smile on my lips was genuine.

Chase took my hand and we headed to his bike. I absolutely loved riding behind him. Since my accident, he'd ditched the truck and had me riding with him everywhere we went. I suspect it was to get me addicted to riding so I put off getting my license a while, but had no proof. Once we were on the road, we headed to the Boneyard.

As I knew it would be on a Friday night, the place was booming. There was a party going on at the clubhouse, but that seemed to be more for the prospects and younger patched members. All the married or attached members were at the bar. The noise drifted outside and was nearly as loud in the parking lot as it was outside the Bones clubhouse during party time. While it was always a good time at the Boneyard, this seemed to be an exceptional celebration.

"Big party tonight, huh?" I grinned up at Chase. He knew how much I'd been looking forward to this. I had no doubt in my mind he was the one to get everyone together in order to make this the best possible experience for me he could.

"Seems that way." I pulled off my helmet and handed it to him as I jumped off the bike and started across the parking lot.

"Wait for me, baby." Chase barked out the command and I stopped automatically. "Good girl," he said with a cheeky grin.

I was about to call out to him that I wasn't a dog

when the screech of tires drew my attention. A dark sedan whipped into the parking lot, speeding towards me, the tires peeling out as the driver accelerated. I had time to scream, knowing there was no way I could avoid the vehicle as I braced for the impact.

Chase called out my name, a sharp, panicked warning. Something hit me, knocking me to the side. A man? We rolled several times before coming to a stop. At first, I thought it was Chase, but he wasn't close enough to have gotten to me in time and was on the wrong side. Before I had a chance to identify my savior, the man lifted me off him by the waist and lowered me gently to the pavement before jumping up and sprinting to his bike close to us. He started it up and sped off after the car.

"Are you hurt, Cotton?" Chase skidded to my side on his knees, running his hands over me. "Talk to me, baby."

"I'm fine. That car was going to hit me." My breath came in gasps as I tried to stand. Chase held me down gently but insistently. "Who got me out of the way?"

"Not sure, baby." We were interrupted when several members of Bones rushed out of the clubhouse, guns drawn. Someone must have alerted them to the incident. When Chase pointed in the direction the car and the guy on the bike had gone, I figured it had probably been him. "One in a dark blue Audi. One on an Indian Scout."

"The guy on the Scout's with ExFil," Cain barked. "If he's on lead, take your orders from him in the field."

Then every single biker in Bones MC took off in the direction of the car that had tried to run me over. Their women were at my side immediately. I looked up at Chase. His face was a mask of fury. He looked at me with such fear and tenderness, but the second he looked away, I could see he was ready to kill.

"Chase." He looked down at me, anguish in his eyes. "I'm fine. Go with your brothers. Do what you need to do."

"I'm not leaving you, baby. You need me."

"You told me what you did before you came to Bones." That surprised him. I could see he had no idea where I was going with this. "You're a hunter, Chase. Your brothers will pull you back before you do something you can't live with. I need you to go find this guy more than I need you with me right now." I didn't. But I knew he needed to be engaged. I also knew that he was the best person to be looking for this guy because he would do anything to keep me safe. He was the one person in my life I knew without a doubt loved me. Looking back, I think he loved me from the first time we actually met. He'd done nothing but protect me and try to help me. Now, I needed to let him help me again even though all I wanted was for him to hold me close. I'd get that later.

"Baby--"

"I need you to do what you were trained to do, Chase. Go find that son of a bitch and make him hurt as much as Cain will let you."

With a curt nod and a hard kiss, Chase hurried to his bike, started it up and followed his brothers in pursuit of my attacker. I hopped he never realized how much it terrified me to watch him go. I wasn't scared for myself. I was fine, surrounded by the women of the club along with the few men who stayed behind, most likely to protect all their women. I was scared for what it would do to Chase's soul. He told me he'd killed, had, in fact, been an assassin. In my book, hunting down someone who'd tried to kill someone you loved with a car then drove off wasn't a bad thing. It was justice. If he did kill the bastard I'd convince him to see things my way.

Chapter Eight

Chase

This ended. *Now.* I had no idea what was going on, but I had an enemy to fight and that's what I was going to do.

The brakes. The fall. Now a near hit and run. One thing was an accident. Two a coincidence. This last was deliberate and that had me rethinking the other two incidents.

No way Tool overlooked checking the brake fluid. Cotton kept insisting she knew she was hit *before* she fell. Could both of those incidents have been an attempt on her life? I didn't know. But the guy in the fuckin' Audi did.

It didn't take me long to catch up to my brothers. I tried to pass them but Bohannon, the bastard, blocked me. Didn't matter much because a short way down the road we found the Audi in the ditch and the Scout on its side with the rider zip tying the hands of the Audi's driver behind his back.

"I'll have all of you little fucks thrown in prison and your paperwork lost! You'll be so far into the system it'll take your lawyer years to even find you!"

"One more word and you leave here unconscious," the Scout rider promised. The man looked vaguely familiar when he looked over his shoulder at Bohannon. "Gonna need a cage to get him back to the compound." He scanned our group until his gaze landed on me. "Your woman good?"

I nodded. "Who'er you?"

The guy shrugged. "Scout. I'm with Cain." That got some chuckles but no other commentary.

"Cage is on the way," Bohannon said. "You know this guy?" He looked at me.

"No. Coward tried to hit Cotton with his fuckin' car. I have a feeling he's been the one behind her recent accidents."

"If that's true," Bohannon mused, "it means he had help getting inside the compound."

"Actually, I'm not so sure about that." Daniel had an alarmed look on his face.

"Explain," Bohannon snapped.

The younger man shook his head once, looking like he knew he'd fucked up and couldn't believe he'd been so stupid, but he did as ordered.

"I found a break in the fence a few days ago and fixed it. I didn't find out until tonight about Cotton's accident. I thought it was just some of the local kids wanting to ride their bikes along the wooded trails. It's happened before, but not since we fenced the place in. I was going to mention it at the next meeting so everyone could be aware and keep an eye out to warn them off." He looked at me, guilt weighing heavily on him. "I'm sorry, Chase. If I'd known about Cotton, I'd've gone to Cain immediately."

I sighed. "Not your fault."

"You did what you were supposed to do, given the information you had." Bohannon clapped the young man on the shoulder.

We were interrupted when a Bronco pulled up and Clutch stepped out. "Told you had some baggage that needed handling." The newly patched member grinned. "I got a nice cushy floorboard just waiting."

"Do you know who I am? You'll all pay for this!"

Scout calmly spun the guy around and cold-cocked him, knocking the guy out. "I told you. One more word."

"All right. Get the bastard to the basement." Bohannon started his bike back up. I wanted to take a turn out here, but knew Bohannon was right. We needed to do this someplace a little more private. "Chase, go get your woman, then come back to the clubhouse. We won't start without you."

I nodded, surprised at how relieved I felt to be going back to Cotton. Cain had put me in charge of the bar to give me something to focus on, but maybe Cotton was exactly what I needed to pull myself above all the bad shit I'd done. Maybe protecting her was my atonement.

Back at the Boneyard, I found Cotton inside with the other women. They'd formed a protective circle around her and were currently showering her with attention and reassurances.

"Don't worry, Cotton." Suzie, Cain's adopted daughter and wife to Stunner, had an arm around my woman, trying to soothe her. "The guys'll find the one responsible for this and crush his nuts." That got a peal of giggles all around. Cotton gave a sheepish grin.

"That's not going away. Is it?"

"It will be legendary," Angel said through her soft laughter. "A lesson to anyone looking to mess with the women of Bones." All the women raised their glasses in a toast, shouting, "To the women of Bones!"

The whole bar raised their glasses with cheers. I just shook my head, proud of the women in my club. They'd recognized one of their own and did everything in their power to include Cotton in their circle of friendship. As far as I knew, none of them knew her past, but I had a feeling these women would celebrate what she'd done rather than look down on her for it.

"You guys have no idea how much this means to me," Cotton said with a smile. One tear slipped from her eye but she brushed it away with a casual swipe of her finger. "It's been so long since I've had friends I'm sure I'll bungle this, but know that I appreciate all of you guys."

Suzie wrapped both her arms around Cotton and embraced her tightly. "We protect our own, Cotton. You've been one of us since you started working here. I'm just sorry we didn't make time to get to know you."

"I didn't want to get to know anyone, Suzie. I was just trying to keep my head down and get through life. What I should have been doing is living it. I have all of you and Chase to thank for making me see that."

"You ladies got room for a guy at the table?" It was time to claim my woman. And to get her away from everyone and have her to myself. I still needed to look her over. If there was even one scratch on her I wanted to know about it. And kiss it better.

"Nope," Angel said. "Pretty sure all the chairs are taken." She spoiled the remark by grinning. "What you can do is take your woman out of here. Pretty sure she sent you hunting because she knew you needed it. Not because she actually wanted rid of you."

My gaze zeroed in on Cotton. Sure enough, she looked more than a little guilty. "I believe that's the first time I've ever seen you lie, Cotton." I rubbed a hand over my short beard. "Now that I think about it, you were shit at it."

She lifted her chin, getting a stubborn look on her face like she wasn't one bit sorry for what she'd done. "Got you to do what you needed to do, didn't it? Just because I don't lie doesn't mean I'm not capable of it. Also, I need to take care of you as much as you need to take care of me. And you needed to be in the action."

I grinned. "That's my woman," I said proudly. "Don't mean I ain't spankin' your ass for it later, though."

"Don't threaten me with a good time." Her cheeky response got whoops from all the women at the table. Suzie nearly sprayed water all over the place but managed to get a hand over her mouth before she did. Angel and Darcy helped clean up the mess with nearby napkins. Everyone laughed.

Cotton took my hand and stepped into my embrace. She wrapped her arms around my neck tightly. I could feel the slight trembling in her body and rubbed my hand up and down her back.

"I've got you, baby. And we got that asshole. We'll get to the bottom of this and I swear I'll keep you safe."

"You don't think all my accidents were accidents. Do you." She made it a statement because I was sure she had come to the same conclusion I had.

"No, baby. Not now. But we're fixin' to find out for sure." I pulled back and kissed her softly to the catcalls of everyone around us in the bar. Cotton blushed but just flipped everyone off. Which got more laughter. So *she* kissed *me*. This time with feeling.

When we parted, we were both breathing heavily and I had a hard-on from hell. She smiled up at me. "Do you want me to stay here with the girls?"

"Only if you want to. I'm going back to the clubhouse for the interrogation. You can stay here where are brothers looking out for you and the other women, or I can take you back with me. But you'll be at the clubhouse. I'm not leaving you at our house alone until this is settled."

A coldness filled Cotton's eyes. It wasn't a look I'd seen before. This woman I could absolutely believe was a killer. Not indiscriminately, but a woman who'd protect her family at all costs. If that meant killing a motherfucker, so be it.

"I want to go with you, Chase. And I want the chance to look that bastard in the eyes. I want to know who it is and why he did it."

"Can't promise you that, baby. But I'll ask Cain. He's made exceptions in the past. Maybe he'll do it again."

"I'll ask him myself," Cotton said with a lift of her chin. If it was possible for my dick to get any harder, I think it did right then.

"Fuck, you're fierce," I whispered. "Gonna have to fuck you soon. See if you fuck as hard as that look in your eyes promises."

"I do," she said, her expression never changing. "But only you."

"Come on. Let's get the fuck outta here."

We rode back to the compound, but when I would have turned to pull through the gate, Cotton tapped my shoulder and pointed on down the road. I wanted to get back for the interrogation, but I also wanted to give Cotton anything she wanted. Given that she intended to ask Cain to allow her entry as well, I knew this was important or she wouldn't be diverting us.

I drove a little way down the one lane road. We were well past where anyone else would be in our path and the narrow, paved road turned into an even more narrow graveled road. There was a section of land on the shoulder that was perfect for a picnic. Cotton and I had stopped there many times and I assumed that was where she wanted to stop.

Pulling over, I shut down the bike and looked back over my shoulder at her. Cotton took off her helmet and dismounted. She moved closer to the little creek that meandered down through the woods and pulled off her T-shirt. Then stepped out of her jeans and panties. I watched in fascination as she removed her bra and stood there in only her shoes and bare skin.

She shook out her long, white-blonde hair, standing there with a challenging look on her face. One hand drifted down her body to her sex, her fingers dipping through her folds. She pulled them away and they gleamed in the fading sunlight.

I got off my bike, removing my shirt as I did so, and stalked toward her on a mission to get those fucking fingers in my mouth. Before I got my tongue in her pussy.

When I was three steps away, she stuck her fingers in her mouth, closing her eyes in bliss like it was the greatest fucking thing she'd ever tasted.

"That was mine," I growled. My anger, fear, and aggression were rising inside me. I had the feeling Cotton knew exactly what she was doing. Probably had the same feelings inside her I did, needing to get out.

"Then you should have taken it," she bit out, lunging for me. She grabbed the back of my neck and fused her lips to mine in a brutal kiss.

I'd never seen Cotton this way. She was always content to let me lead, but this was different. She needed something and I was helpless to do anything but give it to her.

Her fingers went to the button of my jeans where she unfastened them and shoved her hand down the front. She cupped and squeezed my cock, stroking me until I was mad with wanting her.

Cotton looked up at me, an almost maniacal gleam in her eyes. "You need me," she said in a silky purr, belying her fierce expression.

"Not like this, Cotton." It took all my restraint to answer her. The second the words left my lips, I knew they were a lie. So did Cotton.

She yelled, shoving me back against a tree. Sinking to her knees, she yanked my jeans down my hips to my thighs before engulfing my cock in her mouth as deep as she could take me.

Never had I experienced anything like this, and I'd received more blowjobs than I could count. But Cotton took me to another level of pleasure. It was brutal. Violent, even. Her teeth scraped over my dick in a painful abrasion but it only added to the intensity she built expertly within me.

Gripping my hips, Cotton took me as deep as I'd go. I felt the back of her throat. And her muscles as she swallowed, massaging the head of my cock. My hand flew to her head, bunching in all that glorious hair and fucking her mouth before I realized what I was doing. Even then I couldn't stop.

I grunted loudly, thrusting my hips at her face. Cotton dug her nails into my ass, kneading like she had claws. The pleasure was indescribable. Any control I thought I possessed vanished like a fart in the wind.

I pulled Cotton up by her hair and pushed her chest first against the tree. She wrapped her arms around the thick trunk and hung on as I shoved inside her in one brutal thrust. We both cried out. Cotton looked over her shoulder at me, the scowl on her face probably mirroring my own.

"Fuck me, you bastard," she snapped. "Fucking do it!"

I gripped her hips and did as she ordered, helpless to do anything else. My mind was screaming at me to take it easy, but my instinct and my body wanted this. I pistoned inside her, fucking her with all I had to give. The walls of her pussy clamped down on me as she reached for her first orgasm.

I shoved her harder against the tree. "You want friction against your clit? Rub yourself against the fuckin' bark."

With a cry, she did. Instantly her pussy spasmed, the strength of her orgasm nearly taking me with her. The second the contractions stopped, I pulled out, turning her to face me. I lifted her and she wrapped her legs around my waist, finding my cock with her pussy once more. I sat her on the picnic table nearby before starting that hard, driving rhythm again.

I wrapped my hand around her neck, shoving her to her back on the wooden boards. Again, the gleeful smile she gave me was maniacal. She reached up to rake her nails down my chest leaving red furrows from the sharp abrasion. I threw my head back and groaned, trying my best to hold on just that little bit longer.

Then, to my utter shock, Cotton swung her arm and backhanded me across the face. Hard. I stepped back automatically, unsure what she wanted. Had I hurt her? Then she grabbed my arm and pulled me toward her, spinning us both until she shoved me back onto the table. I scooted back when she climbed up to straddle me, guiding my cock inside her from behind. The look of bliss on her face as she sank over me made my dick ache to fill her with hot, sticky cum. I wanted to mark her. Claim her. Make her mine for the rest of our lives.

Again, I grabbed her throat and she lifted her chin, giving me access. I pulled her down for a kiss, thrusting my tongue deep. She moaned into my mouth as she continued fucking me with harder and harder movements. Her hips bucked, driving me fucking crazy! All that hair of hers floated around us like a cape. It moved across my face and chest in the breeze, adding an erotic tickle to our fucking.

Then I planted my heels on the table and surged up inside her, pounding into her with all the force I could muster. I gave a sharp yell as I neared the point of no return, hoping and praying she was there with me. Her scream of pleasure told me she was, as did her clutching pussy.

With a savage roar, I arched my back, driving into her once more with every ounce of strength I possessed. My cum exploded from my dick, filling her as she gave another cry, her breasts thrust outward as she threw her had back. I sat up, taking one puckered nipple into my mouth and sucking hard, nipping it when I felt her pussy spasm around my cock once again.

Then it was over. We sat there, both of us panting and coated in sweat. Cotton leaned her head against my shoulder. I could fee little butterfly kisses against my neck as she praised me. At least, I hope that was what she was doing.

"I didn't hurt you, did I?" My words were a hoarse whisper. I was more spent that I could ever remember being after sex. Weak as a kitten.

"No, Chase. You gave me exactly what we both needed and I love you for it."

"I love you so fuckin' much, Cotton," I confessed. "Hurt so much with it I can't imagine my life without you."

"Me neither." I could feel her smile against my shoulder. "We should probably head back. If anyone happened to've heard us, they'd be in for a shock when they came to investigate."

I barked out a laugh. "That they would, baby. That they would."

"You ready for this?" She pulled back to look at me, cupping my face with her small hand.

"I'm ready, baby. Didn't realize how much I needed this until I was fuckin' the shit outta you and couldn't figure out how it'd started." I grinned at her and she pulled me in for a soft kiss.

"Thank you, Chase. For taking a chance on me."

"Honey, I never gave two shits about your past other than to need to know what motherfucker I needed to kill. I knew you were a battered woman. Just thought it was a man rather than your experiences in prison. Knew there was something different about you when you had Butch by the balls. Wanted you right then. Wanted you before but the way you handled yourself with that lot gave me a hard-on."

"You're turned on when I get aggressive." She grinned.

"Oh yeah, baby. Won't deny that."

We dressed and headed back to the compound. I knew whatever I found there was going to shed light on everything that had happened since Cotton's car wreck. The only question was the degree of beating the fucker in the interrogation room got.

Chapter Nine

Chase

Getting Cotton into the club's interrogation room wasn't as easy as I'd first thought it would be.

"Out of the question," Cain said sternly, his arms over his chest and a haunted look in his eyes, though he tried to hide it. "I'm not lettin' one of our women in this room again as long as I live." He poked a finger in Chase's chest. "You know better than to ask me that fuckin' question!"

"I have no intention of letting her be here for all of it, but she wants to look this guy in the eyes and I think she deserves that much."

Cain shook his head. "I'll take a fuckin' picture of him to see if she can identify the bastard, but she's not setting one foot inside that room."

"It's OK, Chase," she said, hanging on to my arm and rubbing it in a soothing rhythm. "I can wait in the common room until you're done."

"I'm not goin' in there without you, Cotton. If you don't go, I'm not goin' either. You give me the sanity to keep me from slittin' the motherfucker's throat on sight."

She smiled up at me. It wasn't a pretty smile. It was positively vicious. "Who says I'd give you that pleasure? Anyone's slitting his throat, it will be me."

"Which is exactly why she's not goin' in there," Cain said with a satisfied nod. Like I'd just proven his point.

"Prez?" Cliff opened the door to the interrogation room just wide enough to slip outside before closing it again. "Sorry to interrupt, but Data and Zora found something you need to see." Zora was Data's woman and she was every bit as good on the computer as he was.

Cliff led the way to what Data liked to call his command center. There were monitors all over the fucking place and most of them I couldn't make out for shit. Some of them were camera feeds, but others had a steady stream of data flowing down the screen. And, of course, there was one screen dedicated to Leather Goddesses of Phobos.

"Whacha got?" Cain asked as we walked through the door.

Data glanced at Cotton, nodding in her direction. "Uh, we have a situation."

"Don't we always," Cain muttered. "What the fuck is it this time?"

"That man we brought in? The one we're about to question? Turns out he's a judge." Data met Cotton's gaze. "The one whose son raped and murdered your sister."

"Judge Blakley." Cotton's words were a mere whisper. Like she'd seen a ghost.

I owed Data a steak dinner for the way he'd phrased that. He hadn't said the one whose son Cotton had killed. He'd turned it around to highlight the crimes the man's kid had committed first. Cotton was still. Other than the hardening of her facial features, she didn't say anything.

"Mother fuck," Cain swore. "Can I not catch a break today?"

"Also," Data continued. This time he grinned slightly before schooling his feathers. "We caught Butch and his buddies snooping around the fence. After Daniel told us he'd found the hole in the fence, Bohannon set up a patrol of sorts. Got the prospects doing cursory checks at odd intervals. Caught the three of 'em about an hour ago. Great timing, huh?"

"I want all three of them downstairs with the other one," Cain snapped. "I'm done with this horseshit. No way this is a coincidence."

"Explains how they knew where Cotton lived. And the attack at her apartment." I wanted in this fight. Just like I wanted in the hunt for Judge Blakley when that fuckin' Audi had nearly run Cotton down.

"Go on," Cotton urged. "Go see what's going on with my life since I'm not allowed." She said it loud enough I had no doubt Cain was supposed to hear.

"Not sure where this sassy side of you is comin' from, Cotton, but I like it." I grinned down at her.

Cain raised an eyebrow. "Oh yeah? Say that when it's you she's sassin'." He pointed a finger at Cotton. "You still ain't gettin' in. My club. My rules."

Cotton, the brat, stuck her tongue out at the president of Bones. Which got an unintentional laugh from Cain. "Send your woman to the common room. Angel and the girls are already there."

"Ain't goin' without her."

"Yes, you are." Cotton raised an eyebrow. "You're going with your president and you're gonna see that those fuckers are dealt with appropriately. Then you're comin' back to me for more of what we did in the woods. Get me?"

"On second thought, maybe we need to send that one to Salvation's Bane." Cain muttered his disgruntlement as he stomped out of the room. "She and Venus can gang up on the men there. Don't need the women here gettin' any ideas."

I kissed Cotton. She kissed me back even harder, then shoved me out the door. "Get your ass movin'."

"We'll revisit this later," I said, trying to look stern. Wouldn't you know it, my lips twitched as I tried to hold back the grin.

Despite the gravity of the situation, Cotton had given my spirit something to hold onto when I stepped into that basement room. They had just lashed Butch and his crew to chairs and gagged them when I stepped in. Butch looked murderous. The other two looked scared as shit.

"Now. We're gettin' to the fuckin' bottom of this," Cain said. "Right fuckin' now."

Judge Blakley had yet to be gagged, but he didn't look sufficiently terrified for me. In fact, the man just sneered. "Every single one of you assholes is going to jail," he spat. "I'll see to it personally."

"Gonna have to be alive to do that," Cain said casually when anyone could see he was anything but casual. "You tried to run down one of our women with your fuckin' car."

He shrugged. "Was an accident. And I didn't hit her."

"Only because Scout got to her in time. Besides. I find it a mite suspicious that you'd removed your license plate."

Again, he shrugged. "New car. Temporary tag must have blown off."

"Got an answer for everything, don't you." Cain was reaching the end of his patience. "So here's what's gonna happen. I'm gonna ungag the other two. The first one who sings gets to die quickly. The rest of you are gonna last a few days."

"I have no idea who those men are," the judge scoffed. "And now that you've laid down your ultimatum, they'll say anything to spare themselves."

"True," Cain said. "Unfortunately, I have just enough information to tell the truths from the lies. For every truth they tell pertaining to you, we cut off a finger or toe. For every lie, we cut off their fingers and toes." Cain grinned at Blakley. "Simple enough."

The judge scowled. "You'll all pay for this!"

"Why do they always say that?" Bohannon shook his head.

Sword snorted. "Yeah, it's either that or, 'You'll never get away with this.'"

So Cain proceeded to ask his questions. At first no one talked. Until Bohannon cut off Butch's pinky toe. Not only did he scream like a girl, but he sang like a canary. The other two added more than even Butch and no one'd touched them.

Everything I'd suspected had been confirmed. Data had done some digging and found out Judge Blakley had called the employer the parole board had set her up with and gotten the owner to agree not to hire her in exchange for a bribe. That had come in a text near the beginning, which Cain let me see. Butch and his crew had been hired to harass Cotton. They'd started at the Boneyard when she'd first been hired. When they'd failed to get her to quit, they'd stepped it up. Which had been what had happened the night I'd intervened. The attack at her apartment had been in retaliation for the botched attempt to get her fired that night as much as frustration on Butch's part.

Then things got real. Butch and his bunch had cut the fence to the Bones compound and siphoned the brake fluid from the car only Cotton used. It had been Butch who'd broken into our home and assaulted Cotton. Just like she'd remembered, he'd hit her, then moved her against the bathtub. When none of that had worked to either kill Cotton or run her off, Blakley had gotten frustrated and taken matters into his own hands. He didn't do any better than his henchmen. Data had found the money trail. A series of cash withdrawals on Blakley's part and lavish spending on shit that was traceable on Butch's part.

Judge Blakley had protested his innocence the whole time until we'd gotten to his botched attempt at taking out Cotton with his car. He'd finally lost his temper then.

"Bitch deserves everything that happens to her! She killed my son in cold blood!"

"And what about what your son did to her sister? And about how you railroaded her into a ten-year prison sentence when she should have been out in four?" Cain had been in the guy's face the whole time. I wasn't sure what point he was trying to make, but it was clear the president had taken personal offense to this guy.

"My son was innocent!" Blakley was yelling now. Sweat beaded over his skin and blood dripped from the stubs where there had once been toes. Sword had taken over and was now starting on his fingers. It was an old technique. But effective when we just wanted to fuck with someone.

"Your son was guilty as the day is long! I saw the report on Cotton and the one on your son. Brandon Blakley was a piece of shit rapist! He murdered that girl because he knew you'd get him off without so much as community service! You both had that history. Him gettin' into trouble. Daddy bailin' him out. Well, you fucked up. You. All those years, had you made him take responsibility for himself he might still be alive. That's on you, you bastard. Cotton served her time. She owned her actions and sat quietly and took everything dished out to her while you sat back and plotted ways to make her life even more miserable. All to keep from ownin' up to your own actions." Cain got right in his face. "Well, now you're payin' for 'em."

Cain backhanded the judge, then took the cutters

from Sword. "I'm sick and tired of men preying on women. We've had more than our share recently and I'm sending a message with this one."

"Cain," Bohannon said, laying a hand on the president's shoulder. "We can't do that. You know it. Take it out on this fuck, but it's cleaned up when it's done."

"Don't tell me what to do in my own fuckin' club, Bohannon!" Cain was angrier than I'd ever seen him.

"Rein it in, Prez." Torpedo was vice president of Bones. Other than Angel, he was the only one who could calm Cain when he got angry. Which wasn't often. Cain was the most levelheaded man I knew. Stunner was at his side as well. In addition to being a patched member of Bones, Stunner was Cain's son-in-law. The big man never said much, but he always stood shoulder to shoulder with Cain. No matter the circumstances.

"I'll take care of it," Stunner said. "I'll send your message."

That was quite possibly the only thing that could have made our president see reason. His head snapped around to Stunner. The big man just looked at Judge Blakley, ready to carry out any order Cain handed down.

Finally, Cain spun around, swearing loudly and inventively. "Fuck you, Stunner!" The other man didn't let his expression change, but I could tell he didn't understand what he'd done wrong. "You know I can't let you do it. If there's blowback and you went to jail, Suzie would be devastated.

"Yes," Stunner said. "Which is why I volunteered."

"Fucker," Cain muttered.

Then it hit me. "You volunteered because you knew if it was important enough for Cain to risk his daughter's happiness, it needed to be done." I grinned. "Good thinkin', bro!"

Cain gave me a venomous look. "Don't encourage him. He's been taking lessons from Suzie in how to manage her old man."

Stunner shook his head. "If it needs doing, I'll do it. No one hurts our women and gets away with it."

"Bohannon and Sword will take out the trash, Stunner," Cain said with a weary sigh. "But Torpedo and Bohannon are right. Tempting as it is, they disappear."

Stunner nodded his head once. "Good. Suzie's pregnant."

Cain stopped dead, the color leaching from his face. "You got my daughter... pregnant?" I almost felt sorry for Stunner. The big man said nothing for a long time. Then he just grinned. Everyone roared with laughter. Cain gave everyone a growl but looked more than a bit sheepish, clapping Stunner on the back. "Just so you know, I may have to throw you another beatin' for that. Not for givin' me a grandbaby, but for volunteering for something like that knowing you had a baby on the way." Stunner just shrugged, not looking intimidated at all.

"Fine then. Get rid of these pissants. Clean up the mess. I expect every single one of you motherfuckers to be at the fuckin' baby shower, too."

It was surreal. We were celebrating a new life while we were getting ready to take four. The irony wasn't lost on any of us. Probably because of Stunner's news, there was no more torture. The deaths were quick. Each of them got a slit throat.

I bent down to eye level with Judge Blakley and

grinned before Bohannon delivered the kill. "See you in hell, motherfucker." Then he died.

* * *

Cotton

The second I saw Chase I knew it was over. He hurried to my side and pulled me into his arms. "Gonna need that fuckin' you promised, woman."

I giggled. "Always. Whatever you need, Chase. I'm yours."

The night was spent in bliss. Chase took me several times and I took him a few more. By the time the sun rose, we were both sated and had fucked the previous night out of our systems.

"None of this will lead back to the club, will it?" I didn't want anyone getting the idea it was my fault and that Bones was harboring a fugitive.

"No, baby. When we take care of something like this, it's permanent. Nothing'll ever be found, and there will be no trace the man was ever here. He kind of took care of that himself when he finally took the step of trying to kill you himself." The second the words left Chase's mouth, a shudder went through his body. Like even the thought of something happening to me was more than he could think about.

"Good. Because he's not worth it."

"No, baby. He's not."

We lay in each other's arms for a long time. I dozed off but didn't quite go under. That's when I felt something slide onto my finger. I stretched and looked up at Chase. He stared at me, his expression blank. Then I looked down at my left hand. A beautiful gold diamond ring rested on my finger. It was a perfect fit. Nothing fancy. Just a single solitaire... and another gold band.

I smiled. "Is this your way of asking me to marry you, Chase?"

"Nope. I'd never risk rejection by asking. Besides, better to ask forgiveness than permission. I might have gotten Data to file a marriage certificate for us. It's kind of already a done deal."

I laughed. I couldn't help it. "Why does this not surprise me?"

"Because you're a smart woman. Also got your property patch on a vest I'll give to you later. Now. Tell me you love me."

"I do, Chase. I really do."

I kissed my husband. And yeah. *Husband.* I liked the sound of that.

Doc (Salvation's Bane MC 12)
A Bones MC Romance
Marteeka Karland

Talia -- Helping one of my students out of a bad situation shouldn't have been a life altering event. But the second Doc meets us in nothing but jeans and motorcycle boots, I know I'll never look at any other man the same way. I knew Caroline's father was sexy, but he's a well-established physician in the community as well as a member of Salvation's Bane MC. As the daughter of Grim Road MC's president, I know that's a line I can't cross. All I can do is look from afar. *Maybe it's time to break some rules...*

Doc -- When my daughter Caroline shows up in a beat-up Ford, I'm prepared to have me a little chat with some boy who needs a lesson. Instead, an angel emerges from the driver's side, and I'm a goner. Of course, life is never that easy. The girl is the daughter of an MC that flies under the radar in the area. Grim Road MC is even more secretive than Salvation's Bane. Whatever they do must be dangerous, because the next thing I know, her dad is telling me to make her my ol' lady. And my wife. Good thing I've already decided to do both.

Chapter One

Doc

I sat in a beach chair overlooking the ocean. The late afternoon sun felt good on my bare chest. The breeze coming off the sea was refreshing as fuck. Neither did much to soothe my simmering temper. My ex was late. A-*fucking*-gain. I'd tried to be reasonable. I gave her everything the court ordered I give her and more. Why? Because I loved my daughter beyond reason and would do anything I had to in order to spend as much time with her as possible.

Beatrix, my ex, used our daughter as leverage to get me to give her whatever she wanted without a fight. Why did the court allow that? Because lawyers and doctors fucking hate each other. Trix had managed to get a judge who wanted to get into a pissing match with the doctor who hung out with bikers. So yeah. Trix had cleaned up. I didn't protest. Not one time. I held on to my temper and let them railroad me into what amounted to a huge financial burden, and I did it so that, when I asked for joint custody, there wasn't much anyone could protest about without looking unreasonable.

My daughter… Her name is Caroline, but I call her Linnie just to piss Trix off. Same as I call her Trix instead of Beatrix. Yeah. I'm an asshole. I hadn't promised Trix a fucking life of riches and bliss. Sure, I make decent money, but the woman spent more than I could possibly make in multiple lifetimes. The only reason she'd served me with divorce papers was because she found out I'd been treating patients at my pediatric oncology clinic and not charging them. To her, that was money for her I was throwing away, and she thought she could force my compliance by fighting for every penny she could get.

The only reason I hadn't completely bought her off for full custody of Linnie was because I didn't want Linnie to think her mother would sell her off if the price was right. Even though Trix would gladly have done just that. As long as Linnie was safe, I'd never cut her mother out of the picture. Not unless that was what Linnie wanted. What my princess wanted, she got.

Linnie was fifteen. Trix and I got married when Linnie was just a few months old. I'd done four years in college before I'd joined the Air Force, so even though the military paid for med school, I had debt in student loans they wouldn't pay. I'd taken a job in a rural area that paid off my student loans as long as I agreed to work in that area for two years. Rural community? *So* not Trix's style. She left, refusing to give me any access to my daughter whatsoever.

It took the court months to resolve that little SNAFU, thanks to Trix's lawyer requesting delay after delay. I'd had to get Wrath involved after that. Thank God I'd been part of Salvation's Bane and had known Wrath before he'd become part of El Diablo's crew at Black Reign. Once he'd taken over my case, he'd had both Trix's lawyer and the judge begging to give me full custody. Trix had blown a gasket.

Once the divorce was underway, I hadn't asked Wrath for more help. Once was enough. I took my thrashing like a man and never spoke unless directed to by the judge. The passiveness with which I conducted myself probably pissed off the judge even more than simply having me in his courtroom to begin with. But I knew everyone in that courtroom other than my own lawyer was hoping I'd have some kind of angry outburst so the judge could make things even worse for me. In my life, I've been many things. Stupid isn't one of them. Even being with Trix, though not my finest moment, I couldn't say was completely stupid, because it gave me Linnie, and she was worth everything to me.

Since then, I'd tried my best not to have anyone from my club, Salvation's Bane MC, or any other club get involved in my personal problems, no matter how bad they were or how much the men genuinely wanted to help me. Wrath knew I had a hard time and had volunteered to get the alimony and child support reduced to a more manageable level, but I'd always refused, telling him I'd call if things got too out of hand. I hadn't called. I wouldn't even consider calling now either except it was later and later every week we exchanged Linnie. Right now, Trix was four hours late.

"Aren't you a little old to be sunbathing?" Trix always had the most annoying voice. Nasally. Whiny. Insufferable. Every time I heard her voice, I had to grind my teeth to keep from telling her to fuck off. Just like now.

I took a deep breath for control and ignored her stupid question. "Did you bring Linnie?"

"Caroline!" she hissed. "Her name is Caroline!"

"To me, she's Linnie. You call her what you want to call her. I'll do the same. Unless she tells me she doesn't like it when I shorten her name."

Trix lifted her nose into the air and looked down at me with disdain. "She'll be along in a little while." Trix gave me a little smirk. "Charles is picking her up from her music class."

"Charles…" I knew perfectly well who Charles Rothschild was. He was the fancy-ass motherfucker Trix was dating who was fifteen years younger than she was. While I could give a fuck about the age difference, he was more than a little full of himself and not very bright. Trix was treating him like he was a mature adult when he wasn't in any form or fashion. From what Ripper had found on the guy, he was currently living off the trust his grandparents left him, his old man had cut him off from other family money, and he had more women than I was sure Trix could have imagined. Didn't matter. What I did take exception to was the fact that Trix had let another man take responsibility for my daughter without informing me.

"Some reason you didn't tell me you were letting Chucky pick her up?" I didn't raise my voice, but I knew the expression on my face, even with my sunglasses still on, would let her know how much she'd fucked up. I used it often with residents at the hospital. The effect it had on Trix was negligible, but she did swallow hard before she found her backbone.

She ground her teeth, not saying anything about my shortening her boy toy's name. "She's my daughter, Jude. I'll let her go with whomever I deem appropriate."

"Uh-huh." I had to use every ounce of self-control not to fly off the handle. I was ever conscious of my temper when I was around Beatrix. The woman could and often did use my words against me. If it hadn't been for Wrath, I doubt I'd have any rights to my daughter at all. "I have two questions for you, Trix. First, isn't Linnie's music teacher that MILF who flirts with all the dads who bring their kids to practice?"

Just as I'd known it would, Trix's face turned a very unbecoming shade of purple, her outrage clear. "Janet Wankum is a very highly respected musician. She's a graduate from Julliard!"

"Second question, Trix." I ignored her declaration and tacked on my nickname for her because I loved that look of murder I knew she'd give me. Meant I was getting to her like she wanted to get to me, which was to say I was making her hate me nearly as much as I hated her. I have absolutely no idea what I ever saw in Beatrix that made me have a kid with her. Not only was she not wife material, she most definitely wasn't mother material. "Who suggested Chucky pick up Linnie at music practice?"

Silence.

I grinned. Yep. Old Chucky was likely wanking Ms. Wankum. God, I'd love to say that out loud! Right straight to her perfectly made-up face.

"Why can't you let me live my life in peace, Jude? Why does everything have to be such an ordeal with you?"

"Why are you four hours late? We've had the same schedule for five years, Trix. You bring her to me here at the beach after she gets off school. On her music days, I take her to practice. I've never let her miss one, and I've never had her there late. Now, over the last two months, you let me have her later and later every visit. What is it you want?"

For a moment, I thought Trix wouldn't tell me what she wanted. Probably out of spite since I'd called her on her bullshit. Then she caved.

"Fine. Caroline is going to turn sixteen soon. She'll be able to do her own driving to and from our homes."

"You wantin' me to buy her a car?"

"And I want you to assume full custody of her." Trix lifted her chin, glancing around her. "In exchange, I want five million. You do that, and you'll never see or hear from me again."

God, it was tempting! I'd have my baby girl with me where I could make sure she was safe -- and be rid of Trix like a bad fucking dream. But that would prove to Linnie her mother didn't care one little bit about her. I didn't want to do that.

"Have you talked with Linnie about this?"

She put her chin up. "It's not her decision. She's a kid."

"She's almost sixteen. It's not an adult, but it's old enough for her to at least be a part of major decisions in regard to her life." I cocked my head and pulled my sunglasses down my nose to get a really good look at my ex. "Do you even care what happens to your own daughter? Are you willing to just... *sell* her?"

Trix rolled her eyes. "You're making way more of this than it really is. I'm leaving her with her father. That's not the same thing."

"It is when you want five million dollars for the exchange."

"So you're telling me your daughter isn't worth the money?" Her sneer told me she thought she had me.

"Not saying that at all. I just want to know how you feel about our daughter finding out about this arrangement. Because I will tell her everything before I agree to anything."

With a shrug, Trix turned her head to the ocean. "She's more work than I have time to deal with in my life right now, Jude. I'm not going to be home much, and I don't want a teenager running around unsupervised."

"Then why not say that? I'll be happy to take her in. I *begged* to take her in when we first split. Why do you want even more money?" I knew the answer. I wanted to see if she'd cop to it.

"The way I see it, you *owe* me that money. If you

hadn't gotten your lawyer buddy involved, the one who is now district attorney for the Palm Springs area, I'd have gotten a fairer settlement from our divorce."

"Try again, Trix." I smirked at her. She was good at bullshit, but I'd always seen through her. I knew how her mind worked. "You got more than you earned. We were only married for nine years. You thought you'd make me take on more work, and you could milk me for more in a couple years, claiming inflation or some shit. The ten thousand a month you get now more than makes up for any hardship you had while we were married. No. You got more than you deserved, considering you quit your job the day before we got married and never worked again."

"You're a bastard, Jude. Always have been."

"Yeah?" I stood so I towered over her. I'd never hurt her, but I wanted her to be intimidated by me. While I'd always been in top shape, since I'd left the Air Force, I'd bulked up from the lean ParaRescue officer to a hulking biker. "How about this. Our daughter is going to be eighteen in a couple of years, and you don't want to lose that income. Sure, you could hold on to at least some of it while she's in college, but Linnie will likely move out on her own and support herself. That's who our daughter is." When she glared up at me, I added, "At least own that shit, Trix. If you're going to trade our daughter for five mil at least be woman enough to admit you love the money more than you love her."

"I hate you," she hissed. "The only thing you were ever good for was the money."

"Fine." She'd enjoyed the sex enough, but I wasn't rising to that bait. "If I do this, you'll give up my last name and take your own back. I'll insist on it." Before she could reply to that, I asked the question I was most concerned with. "Now, where's your fuckin' pretty boy and my daughter?"

She huffed but took out her phone and shot off a text. Presumably to Chucky. I scanned the parking lot behind us, looking for my daughter. I always kept Trix in my line of sight because that bitch was as likely to try to kill me and collect Linnie's inheritance as she was anything else.

Fifteen minutes later, Chucky still hadn't answered her text, and Linnie hadn't answered mine. Not surprising, since Trix took every phone I gave her and pawned them. Linnie had a burner phone for emergencies, but if she wasn't in trouble, she might not even have it on.

"I swear to God, Trix, if something has happened to Linnie…"

"She's fine, Jude," Trix snapped at me. But her brows were knitted together, and she was calling Chucky over and over. Apparently it was going straight to voicemail.

"Dad!" Linnie called out to me from the parking lot. I hadn't noticed her right away because the car she got out of wasn't the car she was supposed to be getting out of. Instead of the sleek red Mercedes I knew Chucky usually drove, she got out of a light blue Taurus. Car had to be at least fifteen years old. Judging by the slight trail of smoke coming from under the hood, the poor thing had had it.

Relief flooded me, but I did my best not to let it show. Instead, I lifted my hand and waved to my daughter, plastering a big welcoming smile on my face. "Hey, sweet Caroline!" *There you go, Trix.* She wanted me to use Linnie's given name? I hoped she never got the song out of her head.

Linnie ran around the front of the car to the

driver's side. She appeared to be begging the person driving to get out of the car. I was prepared for some sixteen- or seventeen-year-old punk wanting to date my daughter. It was bound to happen sooner or later, though I'd hoped she'd be at least forty when it did. What I wasn't prepared for was the slender beauty who stood and allowed Linnie to snag her hand and lead her toward me. Wasn't expecting this. If this was Linnie's girlfriend, I was so fucking fucked, because I was sure it was bad form for a man to lust after his daughter's girlfriend.

The woman was young. Probably barely out of her teens, if that. She had long, jet-black hair that hung down her back in tight spirals, shimmering with bluish-silver highlights in the sun. The breeze blowing off the sea made all that shining silk blow to one side and whip around her body with every sudden gust. Her skin was pale, a sharp contrast to the gleaming ebony hair. She wore pink shorts with large yellow flowers on them and a short-sleeved white T-shirt. The same flower in pink was inlaid with a smaller, identical flower in yellow. Definitely one of Linnie's friends, romantic or otherwise. Which meant I needed to look the fuck away. Because, no matter how young she looked or dressed, something in me noticed the woman beneath. Even if she was trying to hide that woman.

"Dad! Dad!" Linnie waved as she tried to run with her friend in our direction. The woman with her, however, refused to follow Linnie's lead willingly. She looked reluctant as hell to come near us. Every now and then, her gaze fell on me, and she'd immediately look away. Kept coming back to me, though. Like she couldn't decide whether or not to be afraid of me. "I want you to meet my teacher."

That got my attention. This lovely young woman was most certainly not Janet Wankum. Which made me wonder exactly how old this girl was. If she were Linnie's teacher wouldn't she be at least eighteen? No. Not necessarily. This was a private music class. This could be another student further along than Linnie helping out Ms. Wankum. I couldn't help but let my gaze sweep over the girl again in a more thorough perusal. Thank God for sunglasses. Surprisingly, I recognized her. Should have by the hair, but she always kept it in a bun at the base of her skull. Though I hadn't known she was a teacher, I knew she was a stellar musician. I remembered seeing her play various instruments from the piano to the guitar and violin. Thought she played the flute too, but I wasn't sure. What I hadn't realized at the time was how stunningly lovely she really was.

Yep. She was luscious, her eyes a gleaming cobalt that seemed to look into a man's soul. Her body was slender yet filled out to perfection. Her breasts were small, but with her compact body and finely muscled thighs, she gave the appearance of someone athletic. Maybe that of a delicate ballerina. Not a musician.

"This is Talia. Her dad's in an MC too."

I'd seen her with the younger kids, helping them with all the patience of a woman twice her age. I'd caught her staring at me more than once, but she never approached me or gave me the indication she was anything other than afraid of me. I also thought I knew her father. Which probably explained her trepidation. If she lived in a biker compound, she'd be wary of another MC member.

"Rocket? From Grim Road?"

Her lips parted in surprise, and her pale gaze met mine briefly before she lowered her eyes submissively. Goddamn if my cock didn't give a jerk.

"Yes," she said with a quick nod. "Rocket is my dad. You know him?"

"I do. Good man. Leads his club well."

"Of course, you know that outlaw," Trix spat. "He's a thug, and that girl is as bad as he is. She's trying to steal Janet's students." Trix lunged for Linnie, trying to pull her away from Talia. My daughter gave her mother an impatient look and shrugged her off.

"Mom, Ms. Janet asked Talia to help. She has more students than she can handle but doesn't want to drop anyone. Since Talia is the most advanced of any of us, she helps. Ms. Janet has us two days a month and so does Talia."

"I'm not paying for this little... *tramp* to sit back and play on her phone while you have another practice session." Trix nearly spat the word "tramp." "You can practice at home, Caroline. From now on, you'll let me know what days you're supposed to be with Janet, and those are the days you'll go."

Caroline looked like her mother had slapped her. "Mom! I can't believe you said that! Besides, I know Dad's the one paying for my lessons, because he gives me money for them every week I'm with him." She stepped away from Beatrix and snagged Talia's hand again. The older girl tried to twist free, but Linnie was having none of it. "Talia is a wonderful teacher. Even Ms. Janet says so." Linnie looked at me with pleading eyes. "Daddy, Talia's not like Mom says."

"It's all right, Caroline." Talia spoke softly, patting Linnie on the shoulder and gently tugging her hand away. "Not everyone understands my dad or our way of life. I'm used to it."

The girl turned to go, but Caroline was persistent. "Please don't go yet, Talia. You promised to eat dinner with us. Remember?"

"I said I'd think about it." She glanced at her watch. It wasn't a fancy watch like the kind that connects to your phone, but one that looked vintage grandma. Tiny face. Elastic metal band. "I'm sorry, but I really need to go." To say Talia looked supremely uncomfortable was an understatement. She wouldn't look at Beatrix at all and only cast furtive glances my way. Mostly she had her head down.

"Daddy?" Linnie gave me a pleading look, like she thought I had the power to keep her friend with us. When my little girl gave me that look, there was no denying her. Good idea or not.

"It's all right, Talia. Trix was just leaving. You're more than welcome to join Linnie and me for supper."

God help me, the girl's head snapped up, and she looked at me with wide, startled eyes before glancing at Trix again and lowering her gaze. "I'm sorry. But I really can't. I was supposed to go straight home. I'll be in trouble as it is."

"I'll make things right with your dad, but tell me why you disobeyed him. Did Linnie ask you to bring her here?" I wanted Trix to hear this. Whatever it was. Because, again, I already knew the answer. It didn't take a genius to figure it out.

"No. She didn't ask. And don't worry about my dad. I'll be in trouble, but I know the rules. I'll tell him what happened and let him be the judge of if I was right or wrong."

"Lia..." I deliberately shortened her name, making it intimate so she'd look up at me again. It worked, though I thought I might fall to my knees the second her gaze locked with mine. The girl was stunningly lovely and so Goddamned innocent I knew I was going to hell for all the dirty thoughts I'd have about her tonight. "Who asked you to bring Linnie to me at the beach?"

"Mr. Rothschild, sir."

Fuuuuuuck.

OK. Couple of things. First, I'd be lying if I said I didn't look Trix's way and smirk a little. I didn't wish her ill, but the woman was a serious bitch and had needed taking down a few pegs for a very long time. Karma being the bitch it is, Trix had cheated on me most of the time we were together. I guess she was getting a taste of her own medicine. If I didn't need to take Chucky and beat the shit out of him for stranding my daughter, I might have bought the bastard a beer.

Second thing? Hearing Talia call me sir hit me like a runaway freight train. The only thing keeping me upright was sheer force of will, because every ounce of blood in my body went straight to my dick. Thank God I was wearing jeans. It wasn't much protection, and I'm sure my cock was very noticeable if anyone was looking, but it was better than fucking swimming trunks.

"Lying bitch!" Trix stepped forward and, before I realized what she intended and could stop her, she slapped Talia full across the face. She snapped the girl's head to the side, but Talia turned her face back to my ex, her gaze calm.

"Beatrix!" I knew better than to touch Trix. She'd find a way to get access to the public camera service and use it against me in court. Instead, I put my body between her and the girls. Caroline gasped, but Talia didn't make a sound.

"Talia! Are you all right? Ohmigod! Mom! Why'd you do that?"

"I don't know what the two of you cooked up, Caroline, but I'm sure that horrid girl put you up to it."

"You need to leave, Beatrix." I pointed to her car in the parking area. "Now. I'll give you an answer about the other in a couple of days."

She sniffed derisively. "In a couple of days, the price goes up. Keep that in mind."

I ground my teeth together to keep from telling her to get fucked. It was definitely time to see if Wrath was still willing to honor his offer of help. And, so help me God, Beatrix wasn't getting another red fucking cent.

Chapter Two

Talia

I was in so much trouble... Not only was I going to be extremely late getting home, but there was no way Dad could possibly not notice I'd been in a fight. It might have been an open-handed slap, but I was sure she'd got me with the heel of her hand. I tried not to react, but it hurt like a bitch, and I wasn't sure how well I managed. I'd have a nice, reddish bruise on my jaw by the time I got back to the compound. That would put my dad into a killing rage. No one hurt me and lived to tell about it. That more than anything scared me. I didn't want to be responsible for anyone dying. Not even Ms. Collins.

"I'm so sorry, Talia." Caroline sounded genuinely distressed. I kept an eye on Ms. Collins's retreating form as she stomped to her car and peeled out of the parking lot. I didn't look back at Caroline. I didn't want to see the pity in her expression. "I don't know why my mom did that."

"It's fine. I need to get going."

"No." Caroline's dad growled the command, and I was helpless to do anything other than wait for his instructions.

His name was Dr. Jude Collins, but I knew his road name was Doc. He was the doctor and safety officer for his club, Salvation's Bane. My dad's club, Grim Road, wasn't as rich or noticeable as Salvation's Bane, but they'd done business together a few times. I knew my dad respected both the club and all her members. He might not like a few of them, but he respected them.

I'd noticed Doc the first time he'd brought Caroline to class. He'd been tall. Muscled. Larger than life. I think I fell for him at first sight. He was even larger now, like he continued to work out even though he was the most in-shape man I'd ever seen. Occasionally, he'd wear a tight T-shirt that showed off his muscled biceps and tattooed arms. Most of the time, though, he was in scrubs and a lab coat, like he'd just left work.

Now, he stood in front of me in nothing but a pair of faded, ripped jeans and motorcycle boots. That bare expanse of muscled, tattooed chest taunted me to touch. He'd driven his truck -- I'd parked beside it -- but I noticed his cut draped over the arm of his chair. He might not be on a bike, but he was every inch the biker. "You'll eat with us. I'll make things right with Rocket. The least I can do is feed you for taking time out of your day to help my daughter."

"It really wasn't any trouble, Dr. Collins. Caroline is a wonderful young woman and one of my best friends. I'd do anything to help her out."

"Doc," he said with a wave of his hand. "And I appreciate your loyalty, Lia. Still don't change what's going to happen. Come on. We'll go to Tito's."

"My car --"

"Ain't goin' nowhere, and I think you know it. When did the temperature light come on?"

"Umm, a while ago, I guess." She hung her head again. Why was this woman so... beaten down?

"Your dad know?"

"No. I try not to be a bother. I was going to fix it as soon as I got paid."

"Bother?" Doc jerked his head slightly, as if he couldn't believe what I'd told him. "Lia, I'm sure you're not a bother to your dad."

"I'm not even supposed to be with him. I was supposed to be with my mom, but she got killed in a car accident when I was thirteen. I've lived with my dad ever since." I have no idea why I let that slip. I knew better than to give out personal details. My dad would be so disappointed in me. My shoulders slumped. Add that to the long list of disappointing things I'd done this afternoon.

"In the Grim's compound?"

"Yeah. He's got a little house in the center of the property. He's never made me feel unwelcome, but I get the feeling my continued presence on the club grounds since I turned eighteen is a source of tension between him and his brothers."

"Because you've not been claimed. How old are you, anyway?"

"I'm twenty-two. I should have moved out four years ago, but..." I closed my lips and pressed my fingers against them to keep from finishing that sentence. How did I tell him I wasn't inked as someone's property, and I wasn't a club whore, so the rest of the Grim Road brothers didn't think I should be living on club grounds? It was a rule my dad was breaking by letting me stay with him.

He'd gone several rounds with the vice president over it too. It wasn't that they didn't want me or didn't love me like a favorite niece. Rules were rules. While they all had their own moral code, they stuck to that code. The only reason Rocket had kept me with him was because of my panic attacks. Most of the club saw it as a weakness, and I couldn't blame them. Any rules they'd adopted for the club would be upheld, whether I was comfortable with it or not. Which meant I had to go. Soon. I was surprised they'd allowed me to stay this long. I wasn't sure I could survive with my sanity intact if I moved out on my own.

I was lucky my dad hadn't tried to marry me off

to one of his brothers. That way I could stay in the club with no fuss. I guess he knew that would be too much for me. No matter how much I loved the men in the Grim Road, I could never be an ol' lady to any of them. They were too much like family to me, and I would be too much of a burden on them.

"Look. I'll take you to Tito's. We'll get some supper, and I'll call Rocket to come get you. The club can tow your car back, or I'll have Red's people take it to his garage."

"The club uses Red's all the time. I can have it towed on my own. No need to bother Dad." I gave him a half smile, still not able to hold his gaze. I ducked my head and used the toe of my canvas shoe to fiddle in the sand.

Caroline frowned. "Your dad won't be mad at you. Will he?"

I shrugged. "He doesn't like it when I don't tell him things. But he's got so much other stuff to keep up with, I hate to bring something else to him when I'm basically freeloading at his house."

"Let's go," Doc said, brooking no argument. "In the truck. No arguments."

He drove a big Ford F-150 with a dual cab. I started to open the door to the back, but Caroline stopped me. "Ride in the front. Dad always has his gear in the back, and it will be crowded." She threw me a bright smile before climbing in the back and shutting the door. Yeah. This wasn't going to be uncomfortable. At all.

We pulled out of the parking lot and headed for the diner everyone on the outskirts of Palm Beach knew and loved. The food was excellent and the service warm and personable. Tito, Elena, and Marge had been there longer than I'd been alive. Tito and

Elena owned the restaurant, and Marge had been with them since they'd first opened. Other servers had come and gone, but Marge was always there.

We had the windows of the truck down, and I couldn't help but lift my face to the warm breeze. I loved the wind. I had no idea why, but it was refreshing and relaxing. To distract myself, I tried to come up with theme music for Doc. What would he sound like if his character were in a movie? He wasn't the hero of my story, so something dark. But he wasn't a villain either. Antihero? I wasn't sure. I was kind of hearing screaming guitars and a deep, driving, heavy bass. I imagined he'd be something of a maverick character. Maybe? Someone who went his own way outside of conventional rules. Whether or not society deemed it acceptable or not. In other words, a biker. Yeah, he fit that role to a perfection.

"What time are you supposed to be home?" Doc's voice made me jump a little. I'd been in my own world, enjoying the ride. I usually ended up in my own head when I sat too long. The world around me either disappeared to the tune of whatever piece I was working on at the time, or a unique soundtrack of my own making. All inside my head.

"Um, maybe two or three hours ago?" I glanced at my watch.

"And you let him know you were going to be late. Right?" I could feel the weight of his gaze. Knew the exact moment he glanced back at the road, then back at me. "Lia…"

"Why do you shorten my name?" I tried to deflect, but figured he was smarter than that. I'd have to revisit it soon, but hopefully this could get us to the restaurant. We weren't far from Tito's.

"Dad does that to everyone. I'm Linnie, and

Mom's Trix."

"I see. I'm not used to people shortening my name."

"It bother you?" Doc raised an eyebrow, like he was daring me to challenge him.

"I didn't say that. I've never had anyone shorten it."

"Answer my question, Lia." *God*, his voice was almost like a caress. If I closed my eyes I could easily imagine him rumbling my name after sex. "Did you call or text your dad you were going to be late?" Should have known I couldn't divert him. If he was any kind of officer in his club he'd never fall for a diversion tactic.

"No."

"Why not." It was more of a demand than a question.

I shrugged and looked out the window. "I tried, but my phone didn't charge last night. It died before I realized it, and when I went to text him, I couldn't."

"Why didn't you ask my daughter for her phone?"

"I didn't know she had one." I tried to shrug it off, but I knew he was frowning at me.

"Did you ask?"

"What's your point, Doc?" I tried to snap at him, but it came out more of a whimper.

"My point is, when you have people who love you, you respect them enough to let them know you're safe."

My cheeks reddened, and I had to blink back tears. Yeah, my dad was going to be worried, but I really had been stuck. "I'd never use her phone for something like that. What if she needs the time on her plan in case of emergencies?"

"She has any problem with her phone, needing more data or whatever, she'll come to me. Besides, that's a shit excuse, and I think you know it. You should have asked to use hers. Or anyone's, really. You keep in contact with the ones you love."

I'm not sure I'd ever been more embarrassed and humiliated in my life. Not only was I stranded -- I'd been trying to ignore the fact I no longer had a working vehicle -- but I'd made a fool of myself in front of a man I'd basically idolized from afar for the better part of two years.

"I'm sorry," I whispered, doing my best to choke back tears. "I'll call him the second we get to Tito's."

He sighed, then did something that completely surprised me. He reached over and gripped my hand until I turned my head to see him. "I'm sure it will be fine. I've got Ripper locating Rocket for me. When I talk to him, I'll thank him for your help. He can meet us at Tito's to pick you up. It's neutral territory for most everyone around here. He'll respect that and know I've not hurt you. We'll wait for him there."

"I never thought of that. Will he be mad I'm with you?"

He shrugged. "Don't know. If it were my daughter, I'd probably be more than a little pissed, but if the guy was doing what I am, I'd cut him some slack."

"I'll tell him you didn't hurt me, only..." I touched my jaw where Ms. Collins had struck me. It was starting to swell, and I was sure there was a dark red bruise starting to form. My skin was so fair I sometimes thought I could bruise from harsh language.

"Fuck." Doc scrubbed a hand over his face. "We'll get you some ice for it when we get to Tito's. I'll do my best to soothe Rocket's feelings on the matter, but we'll figure it out. He needs a pound of flesh, I'll let him have it."

"Dad!" Caroline sounded distressed. I turned to glance back at her. Her eyes were wide with shock. "You can't let him hurt you for something Mom did! I'll tell him it was Mom!"

"You'll do exactly what I tell you to, Linnie. You know the rules when there are other clubs around. This will be quick and congenial. If it's not, we'll deal with it."

"I'm so sorry." I was rolling toward a full-on cry, but I refused to let tears fall now. Not with this man as witness. My pride was all I had left.

"No need to be sorry. I do have some more questions for you, though."

I figured I owed him for trying to take care of me. I still wasn't sure how Dad was going to take this. "I'll do the best I can. I won't betray Dad's club."

He raised an eyebrow and glanced at me. "Never thought you would. But that's part of what I mean. You seem scared or resigned to face your dad. Do you think he'll hurt you?"

"No. He'll be disappointed. That's bad enough."

"What about the rest of the club? You talk like you really like them, but you seem like you're beaten down. I don't want to take you back to a bad situation, Lia. If you're afraid of them, I'll make sure you're safe at Bane."

"It's not that. They believe in following the rules. Not necessarily other people's rules, but the rules governing their club." I glanced to the side, because I knew Caroline was listening and didn't want to say anything not appropriate for her ears. "Women are allowed in the club only under certain circumstances. Once I turned eighteen, I was still the president's daughter, but I was also an unattached woman."

"I understand." He nodded at me, and I thought he might get it. He'd probably make me spell it out when Caroline wasn't there to listen, but he was also letting it go for now. "And you don't want to move out... why? If he knew you had to move, wouldn't Rocket have set you up with a place away from the compound?"

Damn, the man was shrewd! "Well, yeah."

"So why don't you want to leave the Grim Road compound?"

"That's not your business."

"No. It's not. I'm still askin' for the answer."

I gave an exasperated huff. "Is he always so obstinate, Caroline?"

"He's not even begun to be obstinate. Pretty sure he could out-stubborn a goat."

"Very funny, Linnie. Now hush." His icy green gaze pinned me before he glanced away and pulled the big truck into the parking lot of Tito's Diner, stopping the truck and putting it in park. "You need me to send Caroline inside the diner to get us a seat?"

"I'm sure you don't want to leave her alone." I was reaching, and I knew it. Not only was I being a coward, but I was going to insult my friend if I wasn't careful.

"She's old enough to go inside without me. I think you know that, too." He didn't look away from me when he spoke to his daughter. "Go on inside, Caroline. We'll be along in a minute."

"Should I order for everyone?" Caroline didn't sound upset. Instead, she grinned at me like she was excited for me about something. It gave me a sinking feeling, but surprisingly, a surge of adrenaline. Like I couldn't decide whether to be afraid or titillated.

"Yeah. Tell Marge me and Lia are having a short chat in private and will be there in a minute."

"All over it, Dad." She opened the door, hopped out, and slammed it shut again before hurrying inside.

Doc turned to me and sighed. "I need to know you're gonna be safe if I send you back. I didn't peg Grim Road as the type to hurt women, but sometimes appearances can be deceiving. Talk to me, girl. Tell me why you don't want to move out even though you're clearly afraid of something."

"I have trouble with... separation anxiety." Hurried through it, hoping it didn't sound as childish as I always thought it was. "The night my mom died, we'd fought. I wanted to go to a friend's. She didn't think it was a good idea. I threw a fit. Told her I hated her. She said we'd talk when she got home..."

"Only she never made it." Doc's hand was braced against the back of my seat. His thumb moved to rub over my shoulder a couple of times, a soothing gesture.

"No. She crashed not even a mile from the clubhouse. I was asleep when they came for Dad. They weren't married. While me and my mom lived away from the compound, Dad always made sure we were protected. More than once I saw members of his club hanging out near our house. They'd always acknowledge me but didn't speak. The only time I had any interaction with them was after Mom died.

"She was supposed to pick me up from Dad's. She called when she got outside the compound. Most of the time whoever was manning the gate would shoot Dad a text. But she didn't come for me that night, and Dad had let me go on to bed. When I woke up, he told me what happened. Mom didn't have any relatives living other than me and Dad, but he wasn't her husband. To make it official, they tried to make me identify her body, but Dad set his foot down. It was the only time I ever remember Dad raising his voice. He doesn't have to. He speaks, and everyone scrambles to do what he says. But he gave the officers what for regarding what he would and would not allow me to do. They either took his word as identification, or they wouldn't get one."

"As he should have. Keep going."

"Well, I guess because of all that, I stress when I'm away from Dad. He knows it, and it's why he insisted I stay with him. I've basically been a prisoner, though. I can't go anywhere without Dad. He has to escort me to and from the property, so I mostly stay inside unless I'm going to class."

"I see." He seemed to consider everything I'd said, brushing his finger over the bridge of his nose. "So it's not ideal for you to stay with Grim Road, but you aren't ready to be on your own."

"That's about right."

"OK, then." He grinned. "Let's eat."

"Aren't you going to call my dad?"

"I'll get in touch with Rocket in a bit. I've got people working on it, so we go through proper channels."

"All right."

Doc exited the truck, prompting me to do the same. Once inside, we went to the table Caroline had claimed. I sat in the booth expecting Doc would sit with his daughter. When he scooted himself in the seat next to me, I looked up in surprise. Doc winked. I didn't trust this sudden change of attitude. The man was up to something.

Chapter Three

Doc

Once I had us settled and we were waiting on food, my phone chimed. Text from Ripper.

Off phone w/yur girl's daddy. Expt call.

It wasn't long before my phone rang. Unknown number.

"This is Doc."

"I was told you had a package of mine." The man sounded livid.

"Relax, Rocket. She's safe. In fact, I owe her a debt. She took care of my daughter when my ex's man didn't pick her up when he was supposed to."

There was a long pause before he acknowledged me further. "I'll meet you in twenty minutes."

"Would you like me to have you some coffee ready?"

"No. And Doc? If you've harmed one hair on her head, there's gonna be hell to pay."

"Noted." I ended the call.

"Dad's pissed. Isn't he?" Marge had gotten her an ice pack for her jaw, and Talia held it to her face.

"Well, I wouldn't say he was happy about the situation." I reached under the table and squeezed Talia's knee once before taking a sip of my coffee. Her eyes were wide and slightly panicked. Her hand trembled when she took a drink of her water. Caroline chatted happily, seemingly oblivious to the tension between Talia and me. I leaned in to whisper to her. "Relax, Lia. I ain't gonna hurt you."

"I know," she said, looking up at me with wide eyes. "I know."

I winked at her. "Good." Caroline didn't miss a beat. She talked nearly nonstop. I've never been so amused in my life. Caroline saw my interest in Talia. Hell, she'd probably set up this very thing. Minus the part where Talia's dad was coming after her. And the part where Talia's car was shit. Worked, anyway. The longer she talked, the more amused I became. My daughter was playing matchmaker. Much as I knew I should be irritated, I found it rather cute. My daughter. Setting me up with a woman. Not just any woman, either. A woman of Caroline's choosing. Yeah. I got it. My heart melted a little.

It wasn't long before a Ford Bronco pulled into the parking lot of the diner. Talia stiffened, her breathing quickening. I frowned down at her. She was really stressed, but why?

"Caroline, why don't you go see if Elena needs help with the cookies in the kitchen." I grinned at my daughter. Marge heard us and quickly ushered Caroline out of the booth and toward the back. I heard something about Marge getting Caroline "the biggest milkshake you've ever seen" and figured I was destined to spend the evening with a teenager on a sugar high.

Caroline slipped through the doors of the kitchen, but not before Rocket entered the diner. The man saw my daughter leave the room before he made eye contact with me. He nodded to me, acknowledging both my presence and that I'd let him see my daughter before I sent her out. Grim Road wasn't a bad club. It tried to stay under the radar, and I was under no illusion they didn't have their own questionable activities, but I didn't believe Rocket was a bad guy.

"Talia. You good?" Rocket held my gaze, not even looking at his daughter.

"Yes. Doc gave me a ride. My car broke down." Lia was obviously nervous. Rocket looked pained at her subservient tone of voice.

"Talia, relax. I needed to make sure you were really OK. When you didn't come home this afternoon, I got worried." Though I wasn't expecting the confession from Rocket, it made me feel better about the situation. Showing any kind of emotional attachment in the presence of another club wasn't something most guys did. Especially if the clubs weren't at least a loose ally. Though our clubs had crossed paths, we were neutral at best.

"I'm sorry, Rocket." Lia spoke softly, looking at her hands where they rested on the table, fingers laced tightly together. It was telling that she addressed her father by his road name. Probably because they weren't alone. "I didn't mean to worry you. I didn't want to be a bother."

Rocket scrubbed a hand over his face. He glanced over at Tito. There were no other customers in the place, so we had some privacy except for Tito, Marge, and Elena. "Can I get a burger, Tito? Maybe some fries and a beer."

"Sure thing." Tito used his spatula to point at Talia. "That one is a good girl. She takes care of Caroline when that mother of hers is so wicked." The older man made the sign of the cross before turning back to the grill to start Rocket's order.

"I know she's a good girl," Rocket said, giving Talia a soft smile. "I've tried to do right by you, baby girl. I know it hasn't been easy living in my world."

"I was grateful you took me in when Mom died. I know it's been hard on you and the club."

"Talia, it's not that it's hard on us to have you around or that anyone doesn't want you in the compound. It's that the men in Grim have their own codes. They don't always conform to society's rules, but they always fall into line with the club's code. Following the few rules the club has is our way of trusting each other. As long as a member follows those rules, he can be trusted within our group."

"And by having me there past my eighteenth birthday violates a rule. I get it. It's just --"

"Hard. Yeah, I know. And you've done everything the club asked of you. You've never once broken a rule we gave to you. It's why you've stayed as long as you have." He reached out and covered Talia's hands with his big one. "Baby, I love you more than life itself, and I'll do anything I have to, to keep you safe. But I'm going to have to move you out of the compound. Tonight."

Talia nodded slightly, her eyes filling with tears she refused to shed. When I turned my attention back to Rocket to tell him to fuck the fuck off, my gaze collided with his shrewd one. Son of a bitch was playing me.

I held the other man's gaze a long time before saying dryly, "Wish I could help."

Rocket smirked, knowing I was playing along. Yeah. I wasn't dumb, but neither was this asshole. "Do you mean that, Doc. *Really* mean that?"

"Just spit it out, you bastard." I was losing patience, and Talia was starting to fall apart. No way I was letting that happen.

"Fine. Tell Thorn I'd like a meeting. I'm proposing our clubs become allies. We don't work for ExFil, but we do work for one of its rivals. I can safely say, while any dealings we have might not follow the exact letter of the law, we try to eliminate the same types of activities in our communities as you do in yours. If our clubs worked together in some respects, it could expand our territories and keep a few more people on the outside of West Palm Beach a little safer than they were yesterday."

"And in return?" I lifted an eyebrow. This was going to be good. And yeah, I'd been prepared for it.

"Take my daughter back to Salvation's Bane. Claim her as your ol' lady. Give her the full protection of your club."

I should have at least tried to pretend outrage, but all I felt was triumph. Yeah, the woman had gotten under my skin. I absolutely knew I wanted to sample her charms. Beyond that? I wasn't ready to say yet, but the sense of panic that filled me every time I thought about taking on a woman permanently -- especially after the disaster that was me and Trix's marriage -- didn't surface. In fact, something that felt suspiciously like joy surged through my chest and lodged somewhere in my heart.

It was ridiculous. I was too fucking old for love at first sight, not to mention too old for this girl. Lord knew the last thing I needed was another woman trying to take me to the cleaners like Trix had done. It was annoying as fuck. This girl, however, I'd gladly give my right nut to have in my life from now on. She was a little timid, but she was sensitive. I'd heard her play the piano. Seen her dance. The girl was magical in that regard. If that meant she was more delicate than the women I was used to dealing with, I'd figure it out.

"Daddy?" Talia sat up straighter, her eyes growing wide with both disbelief and fear. There was a fine tremor in her voice.

"Talia, honey --" Rocket stopped abruptly, his eyes narrowing in anger before he turned his attention back to me. "If you're the one who hit Talia, Doc, I'll fuckin' bury you." Rarely had I ever seen a man as angry as Rocket was now. His hand went to Talia's face gently, turning it this way and that, getting a good look at the bruise my ex had put on her jaw.

"It wasn't him, Daddy. It was Caroline's mom. She slapped me but caught my jaw with the heel of her hand. I knew it would bruise. It's sore, but nothing that will leave a permanent scar."

"And you didn't stop your bitch from hittin' my daughter?" His voice was a low growl. A lion getting ready to pounce.

"Didn't see it comin'. When it happened, I got between the two of them." I didn't really care if the bastard believed me or not but was curious to see what happened next.

"He's telling the truth, Dad." Talia had abandoned all pretext of calling him by his road name. "It wasn't his fault."

Rocket looked from Talia to me several times before focusing on me again. "Can you arrange a meeting?"

"Why me?" I asked Rocket.

"You might not be a high-ranking officer in Bane, but you're still an officer. That will give her the protection of your club. You're also a doctor, well-established in the community. If she needs social interaction outside the club, you have a high enough social standing to give her the respect of the community, so she can do whatever she wants. Go wherever she wants to go. I want her to have the best of both worlds, and that's something I can't give her. It's one of the reasons I've not tried to pair her up with a member of my club. She wasn't supposed to be the daughter of an MC president. She was supposed to have a normal life with her mother."

"Sounds to me like you're getting more out of this than Bane, but the bait is very tempting." I moved my arm across Talia's shoulders. When she sucked in a breath to speak, I tapped her shoulder with my finger, and she hushed. "Before I consider this, I'm going to have to talk with her and Thorn. Her because I'm not going to take a woman against her will. Thorn because this is the kind of situation he and the VP will want to discuss before taking the vote to church."

"I understand."

"In the meantime, I'll take her with me and assume responsibility for her safety and care until I can talk to Thorn. It might be a few days, but I'll make sure she keeps in contact with you."

"I'm good with that. I realize I'm the one who brought this up, but I'm still warnin' you not to hurt her."

It was time to turn the tables on the bastard. "You know she feels guilty for not moving out of your compound. She feels like she put discord in the club. Probably thinks some of the members dislike her very much and might see her as a threat." She hadn't said that, but I wanted to know Rocket's thoughts on this. It was very possible there could be more than one of them angry enough to fix the situation themselves.

"Fuck." Rocket stared out the window for a long moment. When he turned back to Talia, there was pain in his eyes. "I'm sorry, sweetheart. None of that was your fault. I understand why you didn't want to move out, and if I'm honest, I needed you close too. Still do."

"It's fine, Dad. I'll figure it out." Lia spoke softly but looked genuinely determined for her statement to be the truth.

"Honey, you know this is for the best. Right?"

"I don't know him."

"So? Get to know him. Talk with him, and both of you lay out your expectations. I'm not saying I'll change my mind about offering you to him, but if Doc doesn't think he can make it work, he's not going to sacrifice himself and make both of you miserable."

Lia looked up at me. The innocence shining in her eyes was a punch to the gut, as was the delicate way her tongue peeked out at me before she took her lower lip between her teeth. "I guess we can talk about it. You haven't been unreasonable since I met you. I'll trust you won't start now."

I couldn't help it. I pulled her tighter against my side and dropped a kiss on the top of her head. "We'll work it out, Lia. Just promise to talk to me. We'll spell everything out to each other, then make a decision."

"OK. I can agree to that."

Rocket stood, and I followed. He stuck out his hand to me and I took it. "Take care of my daughter. And I mean that in all seriousness."

"I know you do. I swear I'll keep her safe. And I will respect her."

"Good." He looked down at his daughter. "You know I'm only looking out for you. Right?"

"Yes, Daddy. I understand."

Rocket shook his head once, like he couldn't believe what he'd done. Then he headed back out to his Bronco and left. I slid back into the booth, and Talia trembled at my side. I was pretty sure she was in shock and coming down from the adrenaline rush.

"It'll be fine, Lia. I promise we can work through this."

"What just happened?" She looked from me to Tito and back.

"I think your papa gave you to Doc," Tito said in a stage whisper like it was all an amusement for him. I wanted to kick his ass, but he was old, and I wasn't mad. I got something I secretly wanted and fuck him anyway.

"I can't decide if I like this idea or not. What a nightmare." She muttered and shook her head as she stared down at the table. It was obvious she was more than a little bit shaken. When she took a drink of her water, her hands shook.

"Pretty sure you didn't mean to say that out loud," I said, grinning at Talia.

"Say what out loud?" She looked adorably confused, then her eyes got round and her lips formed an O of surprise. "Ohmigod! I can't believe I said that!"

I chuckled lightly. "You know, this doesn't have to be a bad thing." I leaned in and ran my lips along her temple before releasing her.

Marge chose that moment to bring out food. "Feeding Linnie in the back with Elena. Y'all take your time." Marge winked at Lia.

We ate in silence for a while before Lia asked her first question. "Why does the president need to take a vote in church about me?" She picked up a french fry and dragged it through some ketchup. She didn't eat it, just played with it.

"Because of the circumstances. I can't speak for the club about forming a loose alliance with another club. I don't think that will be an issue, because the main reason Rocket wants that alliance is to be able to have contact with you and to watch over you. Thorn isn't going to like having big brother over our shoulder, but I think he and Rocket will be able to work out something to keep your daddy happy." I nodded at her food. "Eat up."

"I'm too nervous." She tried to flash a grin, but there were tears in her eyes. "I can't believe I sat there and let him do this. I'm so sorry, Doc. I've managed to get you caught up in my mess without even trying."

"Honey, you didn't do this. I did. Me and your father."

"What?" She looked adorably confused. God, I wanted to kiss that look right off her face.

"You don't honestly think your dad was really gonna kick you out of the compound so abruptly. Or at all, really."

"But he said --"

"That was for show. Your dad and I sized each other up the second we met. I guarantee you he's looked at me as thoroughly as Ripper's looked into him for me. He knew what he was doing and challenged me to tell him no."

"I hate games," she muttered, looking down at her plate. She put down the fry she'd been toying with and reached for her water again, taking a healthy pull. "I was never any good at them." When she set her glass down, her fingers drummed on the table absently. That was when I realized she was playing a keyboard in her head. It was likely how she soothed herself when she was stressed. Made sense.

"No one said you had to be. He made up that shit to shock you, so you wouldn't protest. Probably figured that if you really couldn't accept it, you'd put up more of a fight. You leave the games to me. I swear I won't steer you wrong."

"If we both know this is all bullshit, why continue?"

"Because he wasn't lying when he said he wanted an alliance with Bane. Which is why I have to bring this to Thorn, and he'll take it to the rest of the club. If I keep you, Rocket will expect certain things. By doing this the way he did, he's guaranteeing you'll have the club's protection, and he can have access to you in case you need him."

"Would your club hold me responsible if my dad did something against Bane?"

"No, honey. Not unless there was irrefutable proof you knowingly helped him. Even then, it would have to be something extraordinary for them to do anything to you. We're not monsters."

"What would I be expected to do as your ol' lady? How long do you think we'll have to pretend?"

"That's the thing. We ain't pretendin'. Your dad specifically mentioned you being my ol' lady, so you'll be appropriately patched with a cut of your own."

"What? But isn't that a bit extreme? I mean, it can be a front or something. Right?"

I frowned. "You have an aversion to being my woman?" If I sounded a touch defiant, the idea of her not wanting to be with me hadn't really been a consideration. Was it my age? Or the fact that my daughter was her friend? Oh, that brought on all kinds of naughty fantasies. Probably the fact that she'd just been sold for services. Yeah. I was a bastard.

"No! It's not that." She blushed, glancing up at me before lowering her gaze once more. "I mean, it would be an honor, especially since my dad hand-chose you with my happiness in mind, but, Doc, I can't..." She swallowed. "That is, will we be monogamous?" I glanced down at her hands which were tapping out a rhythm on the table. She noticed me watching and put her hands in her lap, not looking at me.

I grinned at her. "What are you worried about, Lia? That I'll share you with my brothers? Or that you think I'll want to be with other women?"

She winced before taking in another deep breath. Then again. When she turned back to me, she had her chin up and, even though her face was as red as a beet, she met my gaze with a defiant one of her own.

"I won't be passed around. I'm not built that way, Doc."

"Did I say that would happen?"

"No, but for such a big concession, having another club with ready access to someone on the inside of yours, you can't expect me to believe my life will be all sunshine and rainbows. But I'm not going to be a club whore."

"Again. Did I say that would happen?"

"Fine. Spell it out for me, Doc." She turned, so she sat sideways in the bench seat so she could face me.

"You've been in a club long enough to know what having an ol' lady means. We might as well be married. Like Grim Road, Salvation's Bane takes their rules seriously. We don't take an ol' lady unless we mean it to be permanent. And I don't share."

"I can't have a husband who cheats on me. It would hurt too much, even if we didn't love each other." Again, her face flushed. She was obviously embarrassed but doing her best to learn the answers to her most pressing questions.

"Never intended on it. I take a woman, it's the real thing. We figure out how to make it work, because you will be my biggest confidante. My friend as well as my woman. We can start out with mutual respect. Go from there."

"No cheating."

"For either of us."

She seemed to think about that for a while, biting her lip as she turned back to her plate, taking one slow bite after another. Once she'd finished all the fries and most of her burger, she turned her attention back to me. "OK. If you promise you won't embarrass me or disrespect me." She shook her head. "I couldn't take being humiliated in any way."

"I swear it, Talia. No one will ever disrespect you, and I'll protect your body and your heart."

"What about Caroline? She'll probably object to me moving in on her mother."

Laughter bubbled up inside me. This girl truly had no idea of her self-worth. "Linnie is pushing us together. Surely you saw that when she did. She set you up good and proper from the second she stepped out of your car. Might not have thought she'd get a chance to disappear into the back, but I guarantee you she'll stay back there until we send for her. She's gonna to be good with this. You'll be good with it, too. Give me a chance."

"What happens to me if your club doesn't approve this?"

"You'll go back to your daddy. I have no doubt he'd prefer it, but he's trying to do right by both you and his club. It might not seem like it right now, but I promise you this is for the best."

"Seems like it puts you out more than anything else. Why would you agree to this?"

"A few reasons. You intrigued me the first time I heard you play. Not only were you passionate about it, but you were exceptionally good. You threw your whole heart into it. You also took care of my daughter even though you knew you'd be in trouble with your father. You're young, but I see a level-headed, determined young woman with a keen mind and gentle soul. When Linnie introduced us, once I figured out you weren't her girlfriend, I knew I was going to pursue you, even if you were a friend of my daughter's."

That got a giggle from her. "Even if I were

attracted to women, your daughter's too young for me." She ducked her head, but I could see she needed to hear this. She seemed eager for acceptance but unsure how to go about it. God, I could see a pleading in her eyes. Something that told me she wanted this but was too afraid to believe there could be a good outcome with this arrangement.

"You're my daughter's choice, Lia. If there is any way to give her what she wants, I'll do it. But understand me. This is not only because of my daughter or the situation your dad pushed us into. I was going after you for my own reasons."

"You actually wanted to... what? Date me? You don't seem like the type of man to date." She gave me a half grin, like she was trying to inject humor into the situation but couldn't quite commit.

"Honey, if the club approves this, it will be much more than me simply datin' you. In the eyes of the club, we'd be married. Since I believe in protecting my woman to the best of my ability, I'll actually *be* marryin' you. That way you'll have a claim on everything I own, as long as you take care of my daughter until she's grown. I'll have Wrath put that in my will. Trix will likely fight you for it, but Wrath will take care of it."

"What? Are you kidding me?"

"I can see this is going to require more conversation than we have time for here. Let's get you settled. I assume you have things at Grim Road you'll want to get?"

"Yes. Everything." Her voice was soft but she seemed to be thinking rather than fretting so I didn't push her. She had to be overwhelmed.

"I can't take Linnie with us when we go get your things. Not until there's an official agreement between our clubs. I'll have to get the ol' ladies to grab you a few things until we can go get your stuff tomorrow. Shouldn't be hard. Once we get settled, you and I will sit down and have a long talk about what each of us wants out of this relationship. You think we can do that? Just… discuss things."

"Yes. Seems like that's going to be important in making this work."

"Now you've got it. You finished or do you need more?"

"No. That's all I want." She peeked at me under her lashes, and her face and neck got red again. Yeah. Her mind was going places she wasn't comfortable with. At least, not yet. I was pretty sure we had a good attraction to build on. God knew why I was agreeing to this, but I knew the second I agreed to take Talia to Tito's I was keeping her. I wasn't sure how until I saw the cunning in Rocket's eyes.

"Good." I dropped some bills on the table and reached for Talia's hand. "Let's collect Linnie and go home. We've got a lot to get settled."

She took my hand. Hers trembled and sweated, but I found it only endeared her to me more. She was sweetly innocent. While I was glad of it, I was also very aware how much was on my shoulders. How willing she was to commit to this depended on how I guided her through being my ol' lady, and how much pleasure I gave her during sex. Because sex was going to be a big part of getting to know each other.

"Don't be scared," I said, leaning down so that my breath feathered over her temple. "I swear I won't hurt you or do anything you don't ask me to. If you'll give me a chance, though, I'll make you glad you gave us a chance."

She nodded but still didn't look comfortable. She

didn't look frightened, just nervous.

Marge got Linnie from the kitchen. My daughter's gaze immediately zeroed in on our joined hands. Talia must have noticed it too, because she tried to twist free. I laced our fingers and tightened my grip. Caroline beamed as moved past us to the door. As she exited the diner, she looked back and smiled at us. Then she went to the truck to wait.

"And I thought things were awkward before." Lia sighed as she shook her head. "This was a bad idea."

"Nope. You don't get to take it back until after we've talked." I tugged her out the door with me, then led her to the passenger side of the truck. Opening the door, I winked at her. She climbed in and shut the door. I'd left the windows down so with the overcast sky the interior wasn't unreasonably hot.

Once inside, I started the engine and took off. The Bane compound wasn't far from Tito's, and I didn't waste time getting there. The more I thought about this the more I wanted it. Looking at the woman sitting next to me gave me a rush. It wasn't her sexual attraction. She was definitely a woman any man would love to have in his bed. It was everything else. She hadn't given me any indication she was interested. She'd blushed, and I could see interest in her eyes when she'd first seen me shirtless on the beach, but that was it. Still, I figured I could get her there. I had to be patient. First of all, though, she was going to be comfortable and feel safe. Not like some dirty old man was going to pounce on her any minute.

We pulled through the gate to the Salvation's Bane property. I drove slowly down the paved drive until the road opened up into a parking lot of the converted firehouse we used as our main meeting area.

"I'm going to find Thorn and Mariana and see if their daughter Sonya wants to go swimming. I'll probably stay with them tonight, so don't wait up. Love you guys! Bye!" She waved before hurrying around back where the families usually entered. Kept everyone away from the club girls. And kept the peace.

"Well, I guess that answers that." Talia glanced over at me. "I guess I shouldn't have worried about her not liking us being together."

"Come on. We'll need to stop by Thorn's office first. Let him know what's going on so he and Havoc can have time to discuss it."

"Do I have to be there?"

I thought for a moment. "No. Not necessarily. Though they will both want to talk to you soon. Make sure you're here of your own free will and that you understand everything your dad proposed and what will be expected of you. They'd never agree to something like this if you weren't on board."

"I suppose there's no sense being embarrassed. I'm sure this happens all the time."

"Does in some places. Not much here, though it's not unheard of."

"Let's get it over with. I hate being uncomfortable." There was a little bite to her voice. Like there was something fierce inside her that wanted free but was a little shy. In the end, she stuck her chin up and clenched her jaw.

"That's my girl," I praised. I snagged her hand. "Come on. This won't take long."

Chapter Four

Talia

"Let me get this straight." Thorn, the president of Salvation's Bane, pinched the bridge of his nose with his thumb and finger. "The president of Grim Road is giving you his daughter in exchange for us being allies? So he's wanting an agreement to... what?"

"I'll let the two of you hammer out the fine details. All I'm interested in is my part in it. Talia. I'm sure he's wanting to be able to see and/or contact his daughter at will, so there's that. You know him better'n me, but he seems like a good guy."

Thorn glanced at me. "No offense, but that will only happen with time. I'm not putting the safety of this club in jeopardy because Doc found a compassionate spot inside him we all thought was dead. You're still another club's property."

"Which is why he wanted me to make her my ol' lady. Then she becomes my property. It won't sever ties with Grim, but they will respect my claim on her."

"You know it's not that simple, Doc. I mean, I get it. But I'm not going to let her loose in the club."

I knew this was coming. Thorn would be a piss-poor president if he agreed to this wholeheartedly from the outset. "I don't have to go anywhere on my own," I said softly. "I couldn't leave my dad's house in Grim Road. Not without him escorting me wherever in the compound I needed to go. He escorted me to and from the gate when I came in from classes. Other than that, I stayed in his home out of the way of the club. I can do that here as well."

Thorn sighed. "It won't be that severe, Talia. Doc will show you the family areas. You're to stay in those sections when you're not with Doc or one of the ol' ladies. I think that will be sufficient until we get this worked out."

"I know this is unusual." Doc spoke softly to Thorn. "Give me time to work it out."

Thorn waved him away. "If you believe she's on the up and up, I'll talk to Rocket. Feel him out and see if there is a hidden agenda. While I object to him approaching you with this instead of me, Rocket and I go way back. Ain't had contact with him in twenty years, but I do know him. He'd never do something like this without a good reason."

"Oh, I'm sure he has a hidden agenda. He's biding his time. Besides, I believe most of his reasoning for giving Lia to me is genuine. I happen to believe there's more he's not saying, and that's OK. As long as he comes clean with you. As to approaching me instead of you, this wasn't a whim, but it *was* spur of the moment. I'm sure he had his intel guy looking into me, but this situation wasn't something he could have anticipated. He sized me up and judged me and Lia's interaction with each other before he made the suggestion. I feel safe in saying the man genuinely loves his daughter and wants what's best for her. He wouldn't throw her to the wolves even to get an in into another club."

I honestly didn't want to hear any of this. It reinforced the idea that I was property, and that any relationship I forged with Doc would be purely transactional. He tried to put a romantic spin on it, but I knew better than to believe that was his only reason. My dad presented this club with an opportunity to see into the workings of a club that might not be an actual rival, but certainly wasn't an ally. Unless he convinced Thorn they could be. Oh well. Nothing to me. I had more important things to think about. Like how far did

I really want to go with this guy? Because I suspected I might let him take me all the way. It wouldn't last, but I thought it only fair that I get enjoyment out of my prison. That way, maybe it wouldn't actually feel like a prison.

"He'll come clean with me." Thorn snorted a laugh. "Rocket always loved his intrigues, but he never let things be so obscure he couldn't get what he wanted." He waved his hand toward the door. "Get on with the both'a you. I'm sure you have things to discuss, and I'd like to have Talia's answer to give to Rocket when we talk."

"Roger that, Prez." Doc stood, snagging my hand as he did. "She'll give you her answer tomorrow."

We headed out the door to Thorn's chuckle. My heart tripped. I was nervous beyond belief. If I agreed to this, what would Doc expect from me? Would he want a real marriage? Did *I* want a real marriage? That was an easy question. I did want a real marriage, though I wasn't sure about Doc. At least, not yet. Oh, I had my fantasies, but how would the real Jude "Doc" Collins compare to the man I'd built in my mind? I also recognized I'd never even contemplate something like this if I hadn't been in an MC long enough to know this kind of thing happened sometimes. While I'd never thought it would happen to me, I should have. This was a way for my father to find me a strong protector. A man he could like and respect. Besides, I had to admit, Doc was a better pick than any of the men my own age I'd hung around in the past. In every single way.

All of this whirled through my mind as Doc took me outside the clubhouse and to his bike. Excitement shot through me at the thought of being behind him on his motorcycle. That meant something in our world. A man didn't put a woman on the back of his bike if he wasn't serious about her.

"Get on, baby." His voice was rough and low. Sexy as hell. I had absolutely no chance of protecting my heart if this went south. And there was a very high probability it would go south. I climbed on behind him and wrapped my arms around him without his instruction. I couldn't help it. Unfortunately, I didn't stop there. I buried my face in his back and... *inhaled*.

God! His scent! Sun-kissed skin. Clean sweat. Gasoline. There wasn't anything not masculine and Alpha about him. No doubt about it, Doc was a take-charge kind of man. I could see it in the way he dealt with Beatrix. In how he'd dealt with my dad. My father had led him to this, had basically forced Doc to take me, and Doc had seen through him. Yet he'd still agreed to this.

When he pulled the bike into the garage by a small cottage and turned off the engine, I asked my question.

"Is this about the club? Are you agreeing to take me in to further their interests?"

He looked back over his shoulder at me. "Does it matter?"

"It matters to me." I felt like I was going to shatter. I was nervous and excited while at the same time terrified I was in over my head.

He swung his leg over the seat slowly. Deliberately. When he stood beside me, he held out his hand to me. "Then no. Sure, some of the benefits the club will be getting are great, but I wouldn't agree to do something for the club I didn't want to do. Not something that involves the happiness and well-being of someone completely innocent. And you're the only innocent party in all this besides my daughter." He brought my hand to his mouth and kissed my fingertips, never taking his gaze from mine. "What I told you at the diner was true. I'd have pursued you anyway. This situation gives me a better incentive to make it all work out to your satisfaction."

I nodded, looking up into his eyes. If the man was lying, I couldn't see it. I saw nothing but sincerity and kindness in his gaze along with a dose of something else I wasn't sure how to name. Hunger? Lust? He looked at me like he was sizing me up. Trying to see how far he could push me before I pushed back. I couldn't have told him the answer to that question.

Part of me wanted to run with it. Follow where he wanted to lead me. Another part, the part that felt I didn't deserve a man like him, was afraid he was using me for his own amusement and would laugh at me when it was all over. Not only was he older than me in age, but in knowledge and experience. He was a strong figure in the community as well as his club. I was a twenty-two-year-old woman with no experience on my own who was basically freeloading off another club. I couldn't survive in the world alone. Mentally, I still clung to my father even though I knew he didn't need me in his life. I was a complication at best. A nuisance was more likely. Would I be nothing more than a complication to Doc once he got tired of me?

"I can see from your expression we have a lot to talk about." He smiled gently as he helped me from the bike. "Come on inside. I'll make us a cup of coffee, and we'll talk. I'll do my best to alleviate your immediate fears, then we'll get some rest. Tomorrow evening, you'll need to give Thorn your answer, but we'll have time for any other questions you think of. He'll have the club's answer soon after, and we can contact

Rocket."

I let him lead me inside his home. It was a bit spartan, the only furniture being a couch in front of the TV and barstools at the island in the kitchen. I assumed he had a bed somewhere, but the place didn't look lived in at all. There wasn't room enough for my baby grand, but I could make do with my keyboard. I had a few instruments I really needed to get, but the main thing I was concerned about was my piano. I needed to play to work off nervous energy.

"You don't stay here much, do you?" I winced. Not exactly smart to insult his home. "No offense," I muttered.

He chuckled. "None taken, Lia. But no. I don't stay here much. I spend most of my time at the clinic. I have a small room there with a twin bed. Not very comfortable, but most of the time it's more convenient than going home when I'm working. It's close to the hospital when I'm working in the ER and lets me keep the clinic open as long as I need to. I'll see about putting a full-sized bed in there tomorrow." He shrugged. "Might be a little cramped, but I'm betting we can work out a way to make it cozy instead." His grin was infectious, but I was so on edge I could do little other than give him a timid smile.

"I won't lie to you, Doc. Not ever." I swallowed, scrubbing my hands down my pants to dry my sweaty palms. "I'm nervous. Not scared, really. Just... I'm in *way* over my head here, and I have no idea how I got myself into this. I'm so sorry. I have no idea why my dad did this."

"He's protecting you. And yes. You're in over your head." Doc smiled at me, not unkindly but I felt the conformation like a punch to the gut. "But you got here because my daughter wanted us together, and because your dad has something else going on he's not telling either of us. He'll tell Thorn when they talk. I know, because Thorn will demand he tell him, but there's no way he suddenly decides to move you out of his compound immediately if it was supposed to happen when you turned eighteen. No. This was a way to push us together without you objecting." He shrugged. "Also, to see how far I'd play along."

"Seems like everyone is managing me. I guess that's the way MCs are. The guys take charge." I knew I sounded bitter, but I was way too much of a pushover for anyone to take me seriously. Especially someone like Doc.

"If that's your way of saying you're not stupid, I get you." He chuckled. A man with most of his face covered in a heavy beard should not look so charming when he smiled. "I doubt your father thinks you're stupid. He didn't want to take a chance you'd balk on him."

"All he had to say was he wanted me to go with you."

"Honey, it wasn't only about getting you to go with me. You had to agree to be my ol' lady. He's serious about that. Don't fool yourself into thinking your dad did this on a whim. I might have been a convenient target, but he's been studying this club for a while. Maybe not looking for a place for you, but for his own purposes. Ripper told us a few weeks ago he'd caught a hacker hanging out in our system and shut him down. It isn't a huge leap to think that was Rocket's people."

"I've heard Rocket tell me multiple times how Crush is the perfect intel officer. Says there's nothing he can't get into given enough time."

"Thorn will find it all out, but I guarantee you, he

has a good reason for what he did. I know it seems like he dumped you off the first chance he got, but he didn't."

"You seem awfully sure." I wanted to believe him. With all my heart I wanted to believe him! Because he was right. It *did* seem like my dad dumped me off.

"If you're willing to trust me with this, I swear I won't let you down. I give you my word. That's not something I give lightly."

"All right. I'll choose to believe you. Please don't break that trust?"

"Never, Lia. I'll tell you everything going on with your father as it's told to me."

"Ah…" I cleared my throat. "Um, what about sex? I mean, you said we'd be monogamous. How soon will you expect me to sleep with you?"

"Hmm, how to answer that?" He grinned at me mischievously. This wasn't at all what I expected Doc might be like. He seemed almost playful. At least, at times. With Rocket, he was all business with no give to him. Same with his ex-wife and Thorn. "You'll be sleeping with me tonight and every other night from now on. As to sex, I'll let you set the pace. Not saying I won't push you, but I'll never be angry if you pull back, and I won't push hard. I don't want you to be uncomfortable."

I shivered. Sleeping in the same bed as Jude Collins? Was I even capable of that? I was afraid I'd make a fool of myself if we did that. "Are you sure that's a good idea? I mean, I can take the couch if that's what you're worried about."

"Nope. You're sleeping with me. That way you get used to my touch, and I know you haven't run off on me. I need to make sure you're safe. Keeping you with me as much as possible seems like the perfect way to solve that problem."

I nodded. I felt like a bobblehead doll. I was shaking so much I probably looked like one. "I guess I can't fault that. But I promise I won't leave without telling you first."

"I like the way you phrased that. You didn't say you wouldn't leave but clarified that you'd give me a warning. I'll do my best to be just as honest as you."

"If you're ever mean to me, will your club ignore it, or will they help me get out of the situation?" I could tell that question threw him. He jerked his head back like I'd slapped him.

"Talia, I would never intentionally harm you in any way. Mental or physical. I know it seems like I'm trying to take over your life, but I promise you, that's not the way it is. I'm going to keep you safe until Thorn finds out what's going on. I'm going on the assumption that Rocket has someone after him, and he is afraid they'll harm him through you. That's an extreme scenario, but I'd rather be wrong than unprepared. To answer your question, if I harm you in any way, you run -- don't walk -- to the nearest brother or prospect, tell them what happened, and they'll take you to Thorn. Thorn will protect you like he protects his own family. He'll get to the bottom of it and always protect you over me regarding something like abuse. The whole club will."

"Wow. That's a pretty strong statement."

"It's the truth. You can ask Thorn before you give him your answer."

"That's fair. As to the other... You should know I've never had sex before. Living in a biker club where you have to either be in your dad's house or with him, I didn't have a whole lot of opportunities to get intimate with anyone. And none of the men there would touch me with a ten-foot pole. Being the president's daughter, they knew they'd get killed if they made a run at me. To say nothing if they'd actually fucked me."

"I can see how that'd be a problem." He put an arm around me and urged me onto his lap. He held me against him, my legs tucked in beside us on the couch, me sitting firmly on his lap. "Like I said. You get to control the pace of this. I'll do my best to tease you and make you interested, but you're still firmly in control. You understand?"

"I do."

"Good. Now. This is the only time I'm going to ask you. From this point forward, if you want something from me, you tell me. Or simply take it. For now, I want you to know I intend to kiss you. If you don't want that, you can get off my lap, and we'll continue our discussion. Otherwise, I'm kissing you as thoroughly as I know how to show you what you'll be getting. Then we're going to bed. After that, it's up to you."

"Oh, God…"

He slowly pulled me to him for that kiss he'd promised.

Chapter Five

Doc

Fuck. Just... *fuck*!

If Talia wasn't the sweetest woman I'd ever kissed, I didn't know who was. She was tentative but responsive to the slow flicks of my tongue over hers. At first, she was completely still, then she sighed and melted against me, opening her mouth to my invasion. She moaned and simply let me have her.

I tried to take it slow, knowing I could only go so far this first time. I wasn't going to fuck her tonight. No. I'd hold her in bed while she slept. Might even make her come. The rest, however, would have to wait. This whole situation was happening. Talia would be mine in every way possible. She'd be my woman. My wife. My ol' lady. I'd told her the same thing when she asked me. I'd never let her go. Her dad had given her to me, and I intended to keep her.

Whatever his reasons were, I seriously doubted he intended for this to be permanent. Even if he said so now. Something was happening that made it necessary for someone other than him to protect Talia, and I'd been a convenient solution. Now that I'd had this brief taste of her, I knew I'd never get over it. All the women in my life, and I had to go and lay claim to a friend of my teenage daughter. I was *so* going to hell...

I could *taste* her innocence! It was like freshly fallen snow. Refreshing, yet so pristine and delicate you were afraid to touch. Her skin was soft and silky against me, her scent wrapping around me like her arms wrapped around my neck. She clung sweetly, her fingers finding the hair at the back of my neck and gripping it tightly. Her sigh was sweet music, as were her whimpers and gasps.

With as much gentleness as I could, I gripped Talia's jaw, taking complete control. But only for a few seconds. My every instinct told me I could take her as far as I wanted, but I'd given her my word. This was all going to be her choice.

I ended the kiss, rubbing my nose against hers lightly. "Now. When you're ready to continue, you let me know." I winked at her, trying to lighten the mood a little without pulling her completely out. "I for one am hoping your curiosity gets the better of you sooner rather than later."

Her eyes were a deep cobalt blue that caught the light, sparkling like diamonds. She looked up at me with lust shining in those beautiful eyes. Dazed. Eager. There was no way Talia wasn't going to be mine. I'd keep her safe. Then I'd just keep her.

"You ready for bed, baby?" I brushed a strand of hair off her face, cupping her cheek gently.

She nodded slightly, her gaze clinging to mine. I could see the exact moment she realized exactly how far in over her head she was in. Talia swallowed. A small amount of fear entered her features, but it was still clouded by the lust.

"Don't be afraid, Lia. Be nervous if you need to -- excited would be even better -- but don't ever be afraid of me. You and my daughter are going to be the center of my world from here on out."

"How can you know that? Any woman in this town would be happy to give you anything you wanted. What makes you think you want me? Because I can't be a burden on you like I've been to my father. That would be too much for me."

"I know, because I've already had more than my fair share of women in this town. And several other towns. Every single one of them had a look of greed and excitement on their faces when I had them in a similar position as you're in right now. Not because they'd found pleasure in my touch or because they loved me. I've always been a way to either money or social status. Even among the club girls. I'm not a high-ranking member of the club, but I have the respect of the community. They think I'll be their key to real power in the city. Or, at the very least, they think they'll have anything they want." I could see her wince, like she thought I HAD lumped her into that same category. Which couldn't be further from the truth. "That's not you, Lia. The look in your eyes, on your lovely face, is wonder and awe even. The truth is, I've never met a woman I wanted to give money or power to. Until I met you, Lia. You? I'd give you anything your heart desired and find more to shower you with."

She gasped softly. "You don't even know me."

"I know enough to know you're a very talented, very sweet woman. I've heard you play more than a few instruments. Pretty sure you dance too. You took care of my daughter when she needed it. That tells me all I need to know about you."

Talia stood, her gaze not wavering from mine. "Then I guess I'll have to work extra hard to prove myself to you."

"You have nothing to prove, honey. Just get to know me. I promise I'll do everything in my power to keep you happy."

She held out her hand to me. "Then I guess we should go to bed. If that's how you want to proceed, we should, you know, get to it." She looked equal parts terrified and eager. I couldn't blame her. I felt much the same.

I kissed the palm of her hand. "You know I'd

never hurt you. Right?"

"I know," she said with a swallow. "I'm just in a new situation."

"If it makes you feel better, so am I." I grinned at her then stood.

"What do you mean? You just said you'd had more than your share of women."

"Not the sex part, baby." I tugged her hand, pulling her against me. Then I scooped her up and strolled to the bed with Lia in my arms. "The whole sharing-my-bed-with-a-woman thing. I never do that. Not for longer than it takes to fuck them, and never in my own bed. That distinction belongs to you now. Only you."

"If you're playing me, Doc, know I'll never recover from this." Tears leaked from her eyes as she picked at my T-shirt collar with nervous fingers. She continued in a voice that was nearly a whisper. "I've dreamed about this since the first day you brought Caroline to class. I saw you, and I wondered what it would be like to have you. It would break my heart if you were playing with me."

I tilted my head at her, trying to process what she'd confessed. "Wasn't expecting that. I wish I'd known. I'd have approached you long before now. But I swear, I'll take care of you, Lia. I told you, I'm all in with this." I set her down gently on the bed before sitting on the edge beside her. "Now. Off with your clothes. I'll get you one of my shirts if you want to wear something to bed. Otherwise, sleep as naked as you want."

She blushed and muttered under her breath about me enjoying her discomfort. It wasn't true, but I did enjoy her blushes. Surprisingly, she obeyed me. I'd catch her if she slipped in her faith in me along the way. And with Trix out there wanting more money, I was sure there would be times coming when Lia would question my loyalty to her. I'd just have to be up to the task. I'd have to wrap her so tightly with myself that she never wanted to be free of me. I'd also have to find it inside me to love again, because Lia deserved nothing less than love from me.

The girl had hit me hard and fast. I'd never been so taken with a woman, especially not the first time I'd met her. As I fetched her one of my shirts, I caught her staring at my body. With each garment of clothing I discarded, Lia watched. I knew I looked good. Muscles and tattoos covered much of my torso and arms. There was also a tattoo covering my back that combined my service to my country, my community, and my club. I kept them above my sleeve line and below my collar so I could cover them when needed. I dropped my jeans, leaving me standing there in only my boxer briefs. By this time, Lia was staring openly, tilting her head like she was studying me.

When she realized I was watching her watch me, she turned away. Hiding as much as she could.

"Look at me all you want, baby. You need to get to know my body as much as I want to get to know yours."

"I shouldn't stare, though. Right?"

I spread my arms. "It's yours. Stare at my body all you want. I like knowing you like what you see."

With a shaking breath, Talia pulled her shirt over her head, then unfastened her shorts to let them slide down her slender hips. Never in my life would I have thought grannie panties could be sexy, but on her, they were like the finest silk lingerie. They weren't baggy, thank God. Me finding baggy grannie panties sexy would be too pathetic for words. They were cut low on the leg and high on the waist, the material fitting close to her body. She wore a white sports bra to contain her small breasts, but she honestly didn't need it. Her tits were barely small mounds, the nipples protruding proudly in an erotic display through the thick material.

Both of us stood there, looking at each other for a long while. Then Talia unzipped the front of her bra and dropped it at her feet. Her skin was porcelain perfection. The contrast between her skin and the inky blackness of her hair was startling. Made me want to taste. I knew I could happily lick every inch of her skin if she'd let me. Especially those little tits. I wanted to suck on those until my eyes rolled back in my head.

Talia left her panties on and crawled into bed, slipping under the covers and lying on her side to face me. I switched out the light and climbed in beside her. I pulled her into my arms so she lay with her head propped on my shoulder while my arms snaked around her, wrapping her up like I meant to keep her. Which I did. The really funny thing about it was, I wasn't fighting it. I was embracing this desire to keep her and keep her close. In fact, there was something satisfying deep inside me that blossomed, took hold, and there was no way I was letting go.

She sighed and slid her hand over my chest to clutch the muscle there. I turned my head to brush a kiss on the top of her head. "That's it, baby. Just relax. We'll get through this together."

"I know." Her voice was almost too soft to hear, but I did. I gave her one more squeeze, then we lay still. I savored the feel of her breath fanning out over my chest. The way she clung to me. The way her scent wrapped around me was a kind of euphoria. I had the woman of my dreams in my arms, and I'd met her less than twenty-four hours ago. Sure, I'd seen her when I took Linnie to music class, but I'd never had the pleasure of being close to her. Now she was in my arms. In my bed. If I had my way, this was where she was going to stay.

I always got my way.

* * *

Talia

I woke up needing the bathroom. It was pitch-dark in the room. Even the window didn't filter any light through. Either there were blackout curtains over them, or it was still night. This wasn't my room. I always left the bathroom light on and the door cracked. I hated the dark.

I whimpered a little as I tried to sit up, but a solid, warm weight held me down. A growl sounded beside my ear and I froze...

And everything came rushing back to me. My breathing quickened and my heart pounded as I remembered where I was and what had happened. I was in a strange man's bed. He was holding me down. But he hadn't hurt me. Right? He'd kissed me. Lord, he'd kissed me! But that had been it. He'd said everything would be up to me from now on. Did I believe him? I thought maybe I might. Gradually I settled. My body relaxed, and the panic evaporated.

"That's my girl," Doc rumbled, nuzzling my neck with his bearded face. "Work through it. Know you're safe."

"I'm sorry. It's going to take some time to get used to." I looked over my shoulder and smiled at him. Doc kissed my nose affectionately.

"I'd say the same for me, but every time I woke up, you were the first thing I reached for. Thankfully, you seemed to sleep pretty soundly and didn't move much."

"I need... uh... you know. The bathroom."

"No kiss good morning?" I couldn't see his expression, but I thought I heard laughter in his voice rather than hurt.

"Is it morning? It's pitch-dark."

"It's about three AM. We've still got a few hours."

I turned my face up to his and reached back to stroke his beard. He took the hint and met my lips for a soft kiss. "There." I grinned, though there was no way he could see me. "Good morning kiss."

His soft chuckle sent a thrill through me, and I shivered. "You like me holdin' you while you sleep? Wakin' up in my arms?" He stroked my face with his fingertips.

How to answer that. "Maybe." My voice was a high-pitched squeak. Though my pussy ached for his attention, I wasn't sure I was ready for that. I was woman enough to admit it might not take much to get me there.

He kissed my neck again. "Go on. Do your business, then come back to me. We've got hours for you to get used to it."

I scrambled out of bed and hurried to the bathroom... except I had no idea where it was. "Uh..."

The bedside lamp snapped on, and Doc groaned like the light hurt his eyes. "To your left. Other door goes to the hallway."

I hurried off. The bathroom was small, but clean, though the shower was easily big enough for two. I took my time, brushing my teeth and running a brush through my hair. I was surprised to find both objects lying on the counter still in the pack. I wasn't sure when he'd done it, but Doc had at least prepared some basic necessities for me. It made me smile and my belly flutter.

When I exited, he still had the lamp on, but I left the light in the bathroom on and only partially shut the door. I saw him raise an eyebrow, but he said nothing. I looked away, embarrassed, but climbed into bed. Doc immediately reached for me, pulling me solidly against him, my head once again resting on his chest.

"You want me to leave the lamp on? I don't mind."

"No. Just the small light from the bathroom is OK. I don't like the dark."

"Don't worry. I'll protect you from the boogie man in the dark." His tone was positively sinful.

"Who's going to protect me from you?" I turned to look up at him, raising myself off his broad chest. When I did, Doc brushed my lips with his thumb.

"You're safe with me, Lia. You and Linnie are probably the only two people in the world I can honestly say that about, but you're safe."

Why I did it, I had no clue. But the next thing I knew, I'd lowered my face to his and kissed him. It wasn't more than a brushing of my lips against his, but it felt good. Not as good as it had before, but then, I was leading this encounter. I thought Doc would take over almost immediately. But he didn't. Instead, he waited until I swiped my tongue across the seam of his lips before he opened his mouth.

He grunted, urging me to continue. I loved the feel of his lips against mine, and there was no way to disguise it. I touched his tongue with mine, lapping tentatively. Doc mimicked my movements, only with bolder strokes. He made me want to do more, but I wasn't sure what I was supposed to do.

I ran my hand over his chest, loving the way the

hair abraded my palm and the muscles played beneath my fingers. One of his big hands found my breast, and he squeezed gently. I knew he didn't have much to grip. My tits were small. Were they too small for him? Would he want a more voluptuous woman? I whimpered as I continued to kiss him, wishing with all that I was he'd take over.

"What do you want, Lia?" God! I loved his nickname for me. No one called me Lia. No one ever shortened my name in any form. I tried not to read too much into it. After all, hadn't Caroline said he shortened everyone's name? Right now, though, I had more pressing problems. Like how was I going to answer that question? "Tell me." His husky whisper was like the devil on my shoulder.

"I want you to take control, because I..." I shook my head before pressing my forehead to his chest. Shame scalded me. How was I supposed to keep this man's attention if I had no idea how to seduce him?

"Are you sure? Because if that's really what you want, I'll do it. Then I'll push you as far as I can."

I looked up at him, unable to keep the tears from falling. Thank God it was dark enough he probably wouldn't notice. "I can still stop you?"

"All you have to do is say the word. Tell me to stop, and I will. We'll talk about why you needed to stop and figure out what to do next."

"Are you serious? That's too much to believe, Doc." I started to pull away, angry that he was trying to play me. "No one's that patient -- OH!" He flipped me onto my back, settling himself between my legs. He rocked his hips side to side until his cock was nestled in my pussy lips through my panties. It throbbed and pulsed against my clit, and I couldn't help the little whimper that escaped.

"I'm not a patient man, Lia. But with you, I'll do whatever it takes to make you comfortable. You are worth every fucking second."

I gasped, looking up at him, trying to decide if he was teasing or not. I couldn't see enough of his face to judge, but his tone of voice was deadly serious.

"I don't..." I shook my head, trying to swallow my pride. "I don't know what to do next."

"All right. Just relax, baby. Let me take over for now. The rules still apply, though. You have to tell me what you want. You want my mouth on you? Your neck?" He nuzzled my shoulder, his beard tickling erotically when he nipped the skin at my neck. I squealed, and he chuckled. "I'll take that as a yes."

Then Doc proceeded to kiss my body from my neck down to my breasts. He took each nipple into his mouth, sucking and licking. Each time he swirled his tongue around my nipple or bit down gently with his teeth, I cried out and my pussy clenched. I know he had to have felt it through his dick. I could feel him pulsing against me. He could probably feel how wet I was getting.

"That's it, baby. Talk to me."

Was he serious? "I-I can't!"

"Yes, you can. Tell me where you want my mouth. Should I kiss you again?"

"Yes! Please!"

He let his chest rub over my tits as he found my mouth with his again. This time, I was more desperate, uncaring if I made a good impression or if I did it right. I needed his mouth... *everywhere*!

"Good girl," he praised. "Now, tell me where else you want my mouth."

"Can't you just do it?" I knew I sounded whiny, but I was past the point of thinking.

He chuckled softly. "Nope. I want you to tell me what you want. I'm not going to sweep you up in this like a whirlwind. This is something we both get to decide. I'll take control, but only after you tell me where you want me to go."

"M-my pussy." My voice was barely above a whisper. I was sure my face was all kinds of red. "I want your mouth on my pussy."

"See? That wasn't so hard, now, was it?"

Thankfully, Doc didn't make me wait any longer. Or beg him. I was afraid that might be where he was headed, but he sat up and pulled my panties down my hips and tossed them to the floor. He spread my legs, running a hand down my belly to just above my mound. His hand was rough. Callused.

"You're skin's soft as fuckin' silk." He followed his hand with his lips, kissing his way down my belly. I thrashed beneath him, unable to stop my cries. "Fuck me! You're so fuckin' responsive!" Though still quiet, his voice was harsh. When he gripped my hips, he did so almost too hard. Would I have bruises in the morning? Did I... did I want his finger marks on my body? I arched my body, crying out again at the thought. That should *not* be sexy. Bruises weren't sexy, dammit! "Fuck!" He relaxed his hold on my hips. "I'm sorry, baby. I promise I'll be more careful."

"What?"

"I'm bettin' I hurt you."

"NO! I mean, the bite of pain is... uh..." I took a breath, fully aware I wasn't making much sense. "You're not hurting me, Doc. I swear!"

"I see." As if he did see, Doc nipped my belly just below my navel. I arched my back, unable to hold back the sharp cry. It both startled me and made my pussy clench in reaction. The next thing I felt was Doc's fingers brushing my cunt gently. He moved them between my folds to find my clit and rub in a small circle. "The unexpected pain turned you on. Didn't it?"

"Yes, but I don't think I'd like too much."

"And I ain't gonna give you too much. Just enough." He licked my belly button once before traveling lower, kissing his way to my mound. Thank God I'd groomed. It wasn't on my normal to-do list since I wasn't dating anyone I'd planned on being intimate with. Now, I was glad I'd gotten the whim. Because the next thing I knew, Doc had muttered another curse and swiped his tongue through my pussy all the way to my clit. "Fuuuuuck!" Then he buried his face between my legs.

* * *

Doc

I had absolutely no idea what happened. All I knew was my face was planted against the sweetest pussy I'd ever tasted. It quivered and wept with my attention, and I had to remind myself to be careful. I could easily overwhelm her. Hell, I was overwhelming myself, and all I'd done was kiss her and eat her out! Fuck! When did I get so soft? OK, that was a stupid thing to say. I wasn't soft in any regard. My dick was hard enough to drive nails. But, God! I'd never wanted a woman the way I wanted Lia.

It wasn't her innocence, either. Though I loved her hesitant touches and kisses, I'd always preferred my women to know their way around a man's body. I found that, with Lia, I enjoyed watching her explore and learn almost as much as I loved watching her like this. Out of control. So caught up in pleasure all she could do was scream.

I felt her body coiling tightly. Sweat slicked her

skin, and her muscles bunched beneath my hands. She thrashed her head from side to side as her hand tunneled through my hair and gripped hard. I'm not sure if she was trying to hold me to her or push me away, but she held on for dear life as I continued to coax more and more honey from her already wet pussy.

"Doc!" she screamed, and I felt her cunt spasm. She clamped down as she came in a wet rush. All I could do was continue to lick her clit, letting her ride out each wave, each contraction. I wanted to be inside her when she came the next time. I vowed I would be.

"So fuckin' beautiful!"

"Oh, God!"

"You wanna come again?" I sucked her clit briefly before she answered.

"I don't think I can." Her body was limp, her hand loosening in my hair. Now she stroked and petted me, like she hadn't just ground her pussy against my face. God, I was so in love it wasn't even funny! How had she wrapped me around her finger so tightly in less than a fucking day?

"You don't, do you? I'll take that challenge."

"Are you going to fuck me now?" I could barely hear her, but the question was definitely there.

"What do you want, Lia? You have to tell me."

"Will you fuck me if I say I want you to?"

"You think I'll leave you like this? Tease you, then refuse to give you what you ask for?"

"I don't know. Doc, I've never been this close to a man before. Not like this."

"You don't want me to fuck you, I'll eat you out until you pass out. But make no mistake. I intend to give you as much pleasure as you can stand for the rest of the night. Whether or not I actually fuck this sweet pussy is entirely up to you. Once I do, though, I'll be lookin' to fuck you often. Not sure I can have you, then leave you alone unless you tell me to."

"I don't want you to leave me alone. Please. Will you fuck me?"

"You asked so sweetly, baby. Yeah. I'll fuck you." I reached for the nightstand to snag a condom. Once sheathed, I lay back on top of her. She spread her legs eagerly, hugging my waist as I settled over her.

I kissed her then, letting her taste herself. She thrust her tongue into my mouth eagerly, whimpering over and over. Her fingers clutched my sides as she thrust her pelvis at me. Yeah, my little Lia was going to be an aggressive lover. She had to find her footing. I'd happily let her experiment to her heart's content.

Moving forward that little bit, my cock kissed the entrance to her pussy, and Lia nearly came unglued. She cried out, tensing up but clutching me to her just the same. With a careful thrust forward, the head penetrated her. Lia's legs tightened around me, her breathing erratic.

"Please," she whispered. "Put it in me."

"You want my cock inside you? All the way?"

"More than anything. Oh, God! Please!" There was an edge to her voice. She was all into this. No turning back. She wanted me as much as I wanted her.

"Take a breath, baby." She nodded and inhaled. The second she did, I pushed the rest of the way in. I was long and thick, and Lia was so very tight. I groaned at the same time she screamed. It took me a moment to figure out she was already coming around my cock and not crying out in pain. The second I realized it, I had to fight to keep from coming myself. Because really. Wouldn't that be embarrassing?

I held as still as I could, letting her finish out her

orgasm before I moved inside her. I started out slow, careful of her untried state. I tried to take my cues from her, but the light was dim, and it was hard to read her expressions. I shouldn't have worried. Lia met me thrust for thrust. Her heels dug into my ass, and she urged me to move faster. Harder. And, sweet God above, I wanted to *pound* into her! To lose myself in her hot sweetness. But I couldn't. Not this time. I had to make sure she got as much pleasure as I could give her. There'd be time for me later.

It didn't take her long to crest again. This time when she came, I joined her. With a loud groan, I emptied myself into that cursed condom. I wanted to fill her up with my seed. To stake my claim good and proper. But, again, there'd be time for that.

I collapsed on top of her. Lia didn't seem to mind my heavy weight pinning her down, though. She found my hair with her fingers again and dug them in, rubbing my scalp in a soothing motion. She whimpered as she turned her head to kiss my cheek. So I met her kiss with my own. This time, I was gentle. Tender. Only wanting to praise, not arouse.

"You good, baby?"

"Yeah." Her sigh sounded happy and content. "Better than good. I've never felt anything like that before. Thank you."

"I'm the one who should be thankin' you, sweetheart. You were absolutely perfect." I gave her a lingering kiss before rolling off her and heading to the bathroom. "Don't move. I'll be right back."

I made short work of the condom and washed myself quickly. Then, taking a clean cloth, I wet it with warm water and hurried back to Lia. She protested slightly, but the girl was already fighting sleep. She let me clean her gently before I climbed back into bed with her. She was utterly still, her only movement the subtle rise and fall of her chest. She'd passed out cold.

With a soft chuckle, I pulled the covers around us and settled myself next to her. God, she was priceless! There was no way I could have ever found a woman so perfectly suited to me. I didn't give a fuck if I was two decades older than her. Talia was mine. Given to me by her daddy, she'd accepted me enough to let me have her body. Next thing I'd do was win her heart. Lord knew she already had mine.

Chapter Six

Doc

"So? What's the verdict?" Thorn leaned back in his chair where he sat in his office. His desk was immaculate, which meant he was expecting company.

Lia held tightly to my hand as we sat on the leather couch in front of Thorn's desk. She looked up at me. When I nodded, she turned her attention back to Thorn. "Before I answer that, I want to know what you think about it."

Thorn held her gaze for several seconds before he spoke. Instead of answering her right away he skipped ahead in the conversation. "He said he wanted to marry you as well to give you the protection of his name as well as financial security. Naturally, there will be loose ends to work out." Thorn glanced from Lia to me. "I hear you have problems with your ex?"

"I do. It can wait until things are settled with Lia and Rocket, though." I nodded at his desk. "You're expecting company?"

"Yep. Rocket and his enforcer will be here shortly. I want this thing settled so we all know what to expect from each other." He pinned Talia with a hard gaze. "You'll stay for this meeting until I say to leave." He leaned back in his chair and scrubbed a hand over his face. "The last thing I want is for there to be any misunderstandings regarding the daughter of the president of another MC. I know how I'd feel if you were my own daughter."

"I understand." Lia's voice was soft but strong.

"To answer your question, you obviously make Doc happy. Caroline couldn't stop talking about you yesterday. She says you're always so patient with your students, and you never hesitate to help anyone. She was genuinely excited for you to be with her dad." He shrugged. "I think you'll be good for the two of them. You'll round out their family and be the glue that holds them together. So, I'm all for it." Talia glanced at me, a becoming blush sweeping up her neck. "So?" Thorn raised an eyebrow at her. "You stayin' or goin'?"

Talia looked up at me with a slight smile. "I'm staying."

"Yeah, I can see that." Thorn chuckled.

"I-I have questions, though." Lia was nervous. Anyone could see that. But she was standing up for herself. Asking the things that were important to her.

"Lay it on me." Thorn grinned as he glanced at me, obviously pleased she wasn't as meek as she'd seemed at first.

"What happens if Doc..." She swallowed and glanced at me. She was trying to phrase her question delicately so she didn't insult me. I knew it like I knew my own name. "I mean, he's been good to me. He says and does all the right things, and I'm actually looking forward to at least giving this a try, but I don't really know Doc. What if he's..."

"What she's trying to ask is, if I hurt her, will you have her back, or will you throw her back to the wolves?" I winked at Lia when her face reddened, and she ducked her head. I couldn't have her ashamed for wanting the answer to that question, so I put an arm around her and pulled her closer so I could kiss her cheek.

Thorn scowled. "He hurts you in any way -- mental or physical -- I'll kick his ass first and ask questions later. The infraction is big enough, I'll kill him."

Lia gasped and turned her head sharply to look at me. Her lower lip trembled, and her eyes glistened with moisture. "No!"

"Hey, now. I ain't gonna hurt you so you don't have anything to worry about. This is exactly why I told you to ask Thorn about it. I knew that would be his answer, and rightly so." She turned her face into my chest and inhaled. Thorn had a soft look on his face as he gave Lia a smile she couldn't see. Yeah, he had my number. He also now knew Lia was all in. She'd be mine even if Rocket changed his mind.

"I guess that answers the question of whether or not she really wants this." Thorn chuckled. "You got any more questions for me, Talia? I'm expecting your father any time now."

She sniffed once, then turned back to face Thorn. "What happens to me if my father betrays you?"

That startled me. "I thought we'd gone over that, honey. You're not responsible for your father's actions."

"I know you did. But I want to hear it from Thorn." She stuck her chin up, her mien stubborn.

The president nodded slowly. "I can see how that would be something you'd want to know. Before I answer, let me ask you a question."

"Of course."

"Do you think your father would betray us?"

She took her time answering, really thinking it over if her expression was anything to go by. "No. I mean, not unless he thought you were hurting someone. I've heard him say often enough that MCs do their own thing. The only thing he actively fights against is human trafficking and some forms of drug trafficking. Says the latter isn't really his business, but he doesn't condone selling to kids. He'd also interfere if he thought you were hurting the women and children in the compound. He can't stand bullies."

"And Rocket doesn't put his little girl in the hands of sex traffickers." I kissed the top of Lia's head before facing Thorn again.

"Makes sense." Thorn rested his forearms on his desk, his fingers laced together as he leaned forward. "If your father betrays us, we will look into whether or not you had a hand in it. I won't deny that or try to make you believe otherwise. I'd be negligent if I didn't."

"Of course." Talia nodded at Thorn.

"But any investigation will be done judiciously. Meaning, we're not going to go looking for ways to hang you. We'll look at the circumstances and your relationship to them. I can even honestly say, we'll look for every way we can to believe you're innocent. If you do assist your father in betraying us, we'll look at whether or not you did it willingly or under duress. Or even if you were aware he was using you. What happens next would depend on that investigation."

"And if you believe I did it unknowingly or that he deceived me into helping him?"

"Then we'll take that into consideration, and you'll give us your account. If you were truly innocent in anything like that, you won't be harmed in any way. But if you're a plant for your father, for his club --"

"She gets it, Thorn." I couldn't hear him tell Lia he'd see her dead if she intentionally betrayed Salvation's Bane. "I'd have to be thoroughly convinced she had an active, knowledgeable part in anything like that before I'd believe it. I'll defend her to the death otherwise."

"Any man worth his salt would defend his woman that hard." Thorn acknowledged me with a nod of his head. "Anyway, we're not going to have to worry about that, because Rocket isn't that kind of president. He doesn't try to take something down from the inside. He goes with a full-on frontal assault. Like a man. Only a coward would use his daughter as a mole. Even if that daughter's grown. Rocket is many things, but he's most definitely not a coward. You're safe here, Talia. I swear it on my life."

Talia looked up at me for confirmation. I smiled down at her. "You and Linnie are the most important people in my life, Lia. I love the men in my club. They're my brothers. But they can take care of themselves. We protect our families with our lives. All of us. You're one of us now. It will be official as soon as Thorn and Havoc discuss it and are in agreement. They'll inform the rest of the club, and they'll vote. You'll receive your patch then."

"Will I need to be inked too?"

"That's up to you. There may be a couple of the ol' ladies who chose to get a property patch inked on them, but if they did, it's not in an obvious place. Mariana didn't get a tattoo. We've never required it."

Talia looked up at me, her expression hardening as if preparing for a fight. "I want to be inked." Unexpectedly, tears formed in those clear, bluish silver eyes. "With your property mark." She shook her head sharply. "I don't want to be passed off again, Doc."

"Fuck." Thorn swore and scrubbed a hand over his face. I wrapped my arms around Talia and kissed her temple again.

Havoc entered the room then. Rocket and another man followed him. Beast, our enforcer, entered last and shut the door. Rocket parted his lips as if to speak, then glanced at me and Talia. His mouth snapped shut when he saw Talia's face. No doubt he saw her tears.

"Who the fuck made her cry?" Rocket bit out. It

was more than I could take.

"You did, you son of a bitch," I snapped, getting to my feet.

"That's enough, Doc." Thorn's rebuke was soft, but there was no doubt he meant business.

"No." Rocket stalked across the room to stand in front of me. We were close to the same height and both bulked with muscle so neither of us intimidated the other enough to back down. Any menace Rocket threw in my direction was reflected back at him from me. "I want to know what he means by that."

"You dumped her off, Rocket," Thorn said nonchalantly, as if he were merely passing along information and not delivering an emotional blow to the president of another club. "Into the hands of men who were strangers to her. Like an unwanted kid headed off to boarding school. You expected her to be happy about that?"

"Thorn, please." Talia stood, her hand finding mine, lacing our fingers together. I kept my body between her and her father, wanting Rocket to understand he'd given me his daughter and I meant to keep her. Even if it meant keeping him away from her. "I'm sure there was a good reason."

For his part, Rocket looked like someone had kicked him in the balls. Pain racked his features, and his gaze fell on Talia with a kind of pleading. "Honey, that's not what I was doing. Surely to God you understand that. I was protecting you."

"Protecting me from what? From Grim Road? Would the men have done something horrible to me?"

"You know better than that, Talia." It was the man with Rocket who spoke. "Every man in Grim would defend you to the death. You're the president's daughter. We'd never harm you."

"But I was supposed to be gone when I came of age." If she scoffed slightly, I couldn't blame her. She was better at holding in emotions than I was in this circumstance, but anyone could see the pain on her face.

The man shrugged. "What's 'of age'? You weren't ready to move out. Sure, we argued about it in church, but that's what church is for. We all knew your background and how you lost your mother. We also knew the incident shook Rocket as much as it did you. The two of you needed each other. We weren't going to kick you out, though I won't lie and say it wasn't discussed. You're still part of Grim Road, Talia. You always will be."

"I called this meeting to discuss your terms, Rocket." Thorn tried to divert Rocket's attention back to him. "Talia has decided to stay with Doc. Once this meeting is concluded, me and Havoc will have a chat, then we'll hold church. Regardless of what's discussed here now or decided later, Talia has thrown her lot in with us. I don't see any member of Bane not agreeing to let her be Doc's ol' lady, even under shady circumstances. So know that ship's sailed. She's part of us now. Not Grim Road."

Rocket was silent for a long moment. He and Talia stared at each other. When I looked back at her, Lia's expression was relaxed, and she held his gaze steadily. If I hadn't already been proud for her to be my woman, I was in that moment. Her shoulders were back, her chin up, and she faced her father and the other member of Grim Road with pride and strength.

I caught Thorn's gaze and smirked. "That's my woman."

Rocket growled while the other man raised an eyebrow.

Finally, Rocket sighed. "This is my sergeant at arms, Dom. He's here as a witness to what we discuss."

"My vice president, Havoc, and our enforcer, Beast. You already know Doc." Thorn waved a hand to the other couch in the room. The furniture was angled so we could all see each other without having to move. "Have a seat." When everyone was settled, Thorn began. "Doc tells me you have some requests."

"I offered my daughter to Doc as a sign of good faith. I'd like us to be allies. We'll have each other's backs and aid the other when necessary." I could tell Rocket wasn't happy with having to do this now that he'd lost his daughter as a bargaining chip. She was solidly in my corner, where I intended to keep her. "We want Bane to keep an eye on our territory for a few months."

That startled me. I could tell Thorn was just as taken aback. "That's a hell of a thing to ask even for a sister club. We're not that. What's the rub?"

Rocket focused squarely on Thorn, ignoring me and his daughter. "I've taken a job for the club. It's going to take every member we have, which leaves our territory unguarded."

"Sounds like you've gotten yourself into a pickle." Thorn gave away nothing. "Not sure what we can do about it. We have our own territory to manage."

"It's important, or I wouldn't have taken it. And when I say important, I mean life and death for some of our family. It's the only thing that could make me willingly leave our home unguarded. I'm asking for your help. Giving Doc my daughter was more about making sure she was safe and protected while I'm gone than about bribing Salvation's Bane into helping."

I heard Lia's soft gasp, but she stayed silent otherwise. Thorn glanced our way but only briefly before he continued the conversation.

"Doc, do you have anything to say to Rocket before you take your woman out of here?"

"Yeah, I do." I stood, tugging Talia's hand so she followed my lead. "Thank you for trusting me with your daughter. I have no idea what's going on, but I respect that it must be major for you to part with her like this. I'll take care of her. She'll always have a home with me."

To his credit, Rocket didn't react other than to clench his jaw. "You truly mean what you just said. I can see it in your eyes. I know Talia teaches your daughter and that she considers her a friend. Did you know Talia before yesterday?"

I shook my head. "You gave her to me, Rocket. I'm keeping her, but not against her will. I'll keep her happy. I give you my word." I stuck out my hand to Rocket. He looked at it for long moments before sighing and taking my hand in a hard shake.

"See you do." He looked at Talia then. "I'm sorry this happened the way it did, Talia. I hope you realize I did this to protect you. I'd never have put you in this situation if there had been any other choice, and not if I didn't believe you'd be safe."

"I know. And it's all right. Doc's been good to me so far. I know Caroline really well, and I can't believe she'd be so happy and wonderful if her dad was anything but a good man."

"You need me, you tell me. You understand? I will always be there for you, baby girl."

"I know, Daddy. Thanks. Thanks for taking me in when Mom died. For making sure we were protected before. I know you did, because I saw members of the club from time to time watching us."

"I didn't marry your mom because we weren't

right for each other. Never because I didn't want you in my life, Talia. There was mutual respect between us, but never that deep, abiding love we both deserved. I never regretted having you, though. You've always been the best of both of us."

Talia addressed Dom next. "Watch over my dad. I'm still finding my way here, so he's the only family I have left."

"You can count on me, little sister."

"Let's go, sweetheart," I said. She was holding it together better than I thought she would, which made me that much prouder of her. "Thorn and Havoc need to get the details from Rocket, and we don't need to be here for that."

"I'm ready." She squeezed my hand and looked up at me, giving me a tentative smile.

As we neared the door, Rocket spoke again. "I love you, baby girl. Never forget that."

Talia looked back over her shoulder. "I love you too, Daddy. Whatever you're getting ready to do, please be safe."

"I will. I promise."

Chapter Seven

Talia

The meeting with my dad had been hard, but not what I was expecting. If everyone was leaving the compound, I could see why he'd want me someplace safe. Which meant that whatever he was doing was extremely dangerous.

"Do you think Thorn will offer to help with whatever Dad is going into?"

"Don't know, baby. That would depend on what's going on. Normally, not. We're not allies with Grim Road, and Thorn wouldn't put any member of our club in danger unless it was something he couldn't walk away from."

"If he does, will he be able to monitor what's going on?"

I thought about that for a minute. "I don't see why not. Rocket didn't indicate he wanted our help in the field, though. He wanted us to take care of the Grim territory."

"I know. Wishful thinking. I don't think I can stand not knowing what's happening. If Dad's going into danger --"

I pulled her in for a brief, hard kiss. "Don't think about it right now. Nothing is happening yet. Let them work it out, then Thorn will tell us what's going on."

"You're right. I'll drive myself crazy otherwise."

"Let's get outta here a while. Maybe see if we can talk Marge into giving us a special." God, I loved this man! How had I fallen so quickly?

"OK. I'd like that." Doc leaned in to kiss my cheek. Which was when I realized he'd kissed away a tear that had escaped my eye.

"Come on, baby." He took my hand and led me

out the back to the garage where all the bikes were parked. Snagging a helmet from a rack on the wall, he helped me put it on, then swung his leg over a black Harley and held out his hand to assist me. "Put your feet on the pegs and mind the pipes. They'll be hot when we get off, so wait for me to help you. OK?"

"I got it." I wrapped my arms around his middle as he started the bike. The roar was loud in the enclosed space, but Doc eased out of the garage, and we were off.

I'd be lying if I said the freedom I experienced while we sped down the highway didn't ease my mind. I found it easy to lift my face to the sun and just... *feel*! It was a joy I'd never expected. I could understand now why Doc wanted to get me out of the clubhouse. It was for this. The man had to have known the ride alone would lift my spirits. He was right. By the time we pulled into Tito's diner, I was all smiles. And yeah. I laughed and might have whooped more than once on the ride here.

When he shut down the bike, Doc was chuckling. "You enjoy yourself?"

"That was amazing! Why haven't you taken me on a longer ride before now?" He chuckled, holding my arm as I got off his bike, careful of the pipes as he'd instructed.

"Little witch. It's been twenty-four whole hours. Ain't been time. Besides, you got a small ride. Not like this is your very first time." He chuckled "I promise, though, it's something I intend to remedy. From now on, we'll make the time every fuckin' day if you want." He stood and reached out to cup my cheek before he leaned in to brush a soft kiss on my lips. "Anything that makes you this happy is something I have to make happen."

If I had any doubts Doc had strong feelings for me, they were now gone. He might not love me, but he was well on his way. I could see it in his eyes when he looked at me, but also in the things he did for me. Like giving me little things because it made me happy.

"Can I tell you something before we go in, Doc?"

He brought my hand to his mouth and kissed my fingers. "Honey, you can tell me anything anytime you want. You good?"

"Yes. But I want you to know that I love you." Before he could do more than open his mouth to say something, I hurried on. "You don't have to say it back. In fact, please don't. Not yet. I don't want it to be something you think you have to say."

"You do know I'm not the type of man to do something I don't want to do. Right?"

I grinned. "Yeah. You don't get beyond being a prospect in an MC if you don't have some Alpha tendencies, I guess. I wanted you to know I'm all in with you. This is the real thing for me. I'm sure I'm caught up in the sex and the way you make me feel, but I also happen to admire you. I know you work with children with cancers and that you help them even if they can't pay you. Everyone knows. I was also already pretty infatuated with you from the first time I saw you with Caroline. So, I'll do my best to be whatever you need me to be, and I'll always take care of Caroline."

Doc kissed me again, this time with a little more heat before wrapping his arms around me in a tight hug. "You're one special woman, Lia. I'm glad you're mine."

We walked into the diner then. Tito waved happily as Marge smiled in greeting.

"It's wonderful to see the two of you again. Have

a seat. Two Marge specials coming up."

"How'd you know we were gonna ask?" I smiled up at the older woman, who gave me a smirk, tapping her temple with her pencil. "I know my customers, sweetie. You two are celebrating, and we're all going to be a part of it. The boys' clubs are like family to us, and we always celebrate with family."

"We certainly are celebrating." Doc put his arm around me once he'd urged me into the booth and sat beside me. "Lia's going to be my ol' lady and my wife."

Marge frowned. "I don't see a vest or a ring. You better not be playing that girl, Doc."

Doc held up his hands. "Everything is in the works, Marge. I promise. She'll have her vest tonight and the ring in a day or two. I only met her yesterday."

Christ! Had it been only yesterday? Seemed like longer. Probably because so much had changed in my life. If it all fell apart today, I'd grieve, but I'd be thankful for the amazing life experiences Doc had given me.

"I don't care if you met her this minute," Marge continued. "If you tell a woman you're going to marry her, you better be prepared to do what you say, young man."

"I swear, Marge. I'll even bring her back here tonight after her vest's complete so you can see for yourself."

"You better." Marge raised her eyebrow at Doc even as she wagged her pencil at him. "Otherwise, your special privileges will be revoked."

"If I don't keep my word on this, Marge, I don't deserve your specials anymore."

"I've half a mind to give you ice water, Jude Collins. Consider yourself lucky this time. There won't be a next time."

I couldn't help but giggle. Mainly because Doc looked appropriately contrite. Doc winked at me, and I laughed some more.

"You like seeing me get in trouble. Little imp."

"It warms my heart to see you interact with the people in your life." I knew I looked at him like he was a hero. I couldn't help it. "Anyone can see you're a wonderful man."

It wasn't long until Marge returned with burgers and fries for both of us, a chocolate malt with extra whipped cream for me and a chocolate mocha shake for Doc. Marge gave him the stink eye but winked at me with a grin.

Doc and I passed the next half hour in comfortable silence. Occasionally he'd lean in and nuzzle my hair or kiss my temple. I laid my head against his arm and rubbed my face along his shoulder like a cat more than once. It felt right. The way it was supposed to be. Never had I felt so completely happy in my life. Not since I was a little girl when my mother and father still spent time together. I found myself anxious to start living in my new life.

I was about to tell Doc when the door opened, and Mrs. Collins stormed into the diner. The door bounced on the wall so hard it bounced back at her. The few customers who were present glared at her for disturbing their meal. Marge pursed her lips and glanced at Tito. Elena came out from the back, an annoyed look on her face.

"You break, you buy, Signora Collins. Only reason I don't throw you out now is because of your relationship with Doc," Tito scolded her, shaking his spatula at her. Beatrix Collins looked as furious as I'd ever seen anyone.

"Oh no." I swallowed, glancing up at Doc. If I'd been able, I'd have scrambled as far away from him as I could. It felt like I was taking someone's man when, from what Caroline had told me, Mrs. Collins was the one who'd insisted on a divorce. I knew they weren't a couple, but I still didn't like this. The woman had a child with Doc, for Christ's sake! What was going on?

Mrs. Collins found Doc a few moments later. "You bastard!"

I must have made a sound because Doc gripped my knee under the table. It wasn't hard, just enough to get my attention and refocus me on him and not his ex-wife.

"Trix. I'd say I was happy to see you, but it'd be a Goddamned lie." Doc sounded weary, but I could see a cunning in his gaze that gave me chills. Whatever was about to happen wasn't going to be pleasant. "Had enough yesterday to do me a fuckin' lifetime."

"I told you what I wanted." She waved a fistful of papers in the air before throwing them at Doc. "You want Caroline with you, you know what you have to do. Otherwise, I don't care how many orders you throw my way, I'll never give her up! In fact, I've got social services on the way to take her away from that cesspool of a compound you've taken her to!"

"Do what you feel is necessary, Trix. But that order is legal. Send whoever you want. It's not going to change anything until after the hearing."

"Caroline is my daughter! You have no right to her!"

"She's my daughter too, Trix." Doc tilted his head slightly as if studying his ex. "Tell me something, Trix. You never loved me. We both know that."

"If you want to talk about this, we can do it at my lawyer's office."

"You're the one who barged in here and disturbed everyone's meal. I went through the court and had your notice delivered. Emergency custody means Caroline will be with me until the courts say otherwise. Now, answer the question." Doc's inflection never changed. He was calm, still eating the occasional fry as he spoke calmly which was so at odds with Beatrix's outrage. I didn't dare move or make a sound.

"No," she spat. "I never loved you. Why would I? You're gone all the time. You don't accept payment for the brats you treat -- which is the reason you're gone all the time! You spent all your time somewhere other than at home. Your daughter barely knows you. Now you're trying to take her away from the only home she's ever known?"

That bitch! She was trying to make Doc look like a horrible person when anyone could see Caroline loved her father. I could see the few people in the diner looking at us with frowns. They were looking at Doc like he was the villain in this story instead of the best hero.

"You're a liar, Beatrix. Either that or you haven't spent any time at all with your daughter." I was livid! "How could you even say that? Caroline loves her father. She talks about him all the time. They're clearly as close as any father and daughter. The man dotes on her, and she truly appreciates everything he does for her! Not to mention, the 'brats' he treats are children with cancer. If he lets his fee slide because their parents can't afford to pay him, that makes him an outstanding person."

"It's all right, Lia." Doc gripped my knee under the table harder, a warning to keep silent. Which wasn't bloody happening.

"No! I won't be silent! I'm not letting her berate

you like that. Not when she's questioning how much you love your daughter."

"Caroline knows I love her. That's all that matters, baby."

"Baby?" Mrs. Collins scoffed. "She's the same age as your daughter, Jude!" She looked from one of us to the other, a horrified look on her face before she frowned angrily. "Disgusting! Wait until the judge hears about *that*! If I'd known you were attracted to your daughter's friends, I'd have divorced you long before I did."

"Who I choose to be with is none of your business, Beatrix." I thought it telling Doc called his ex by her full name. The only time he'd done that in my hearing was when she'd slapped me at the beach, and he'd stepped between us. Likely his signal she'd gone too far and he was taking over the situation.

"It is when you're obviously bedding a girl instead of a woman." When the whole of the diner gave Doc disapproving looks, I wanted to claw the woman's eyes out. Doc still gripped my knee, giving it one more small squeeze.

"I have no idea what you think you're gonna accomplish here. This isn't the court. Now. Since I was obviously a bastard, why did you stay with me for eight years when you never loved me, Trix? I was never around. You accused me of neglecting our daughter, yet you stuck around for the better part of her life. What changed?"

"I got tired of your bullshit. What woman wouldn't? I wanted a better life for my daughter."

"Our daughter has anything and everything she wants. Always has. She's not been neglected. She knows me well enough to throw me and Lia together when she could have kept us apart with a simple word to me. That girl loves Lia as much as I do, and that's saying something."

"Love," Mrs. Collins sneered. "Do you even know what love is?"

Doc shrugged. "I thought I did. Now I know I was wrong." Doc shook his head and chuckled. "All those years I tried to convince myself I loved you. I didn't. I had no clue what it meant to love a woman until I met Talia." A shrewd look came over Doc's face, and he sat back, moving his hand from my knee to drape his arm over my shoulders. "If you won't own up to why you wanted to be with me, I'll come clean." He sighed. "I was in love with the idea of you. You found out you were pregnant, and I latched on to the thought of having a family. A child who loved and adored me as much as I did her. I got that part of my dream. You, however... I admit, those first years, I worked a lot. Why? To try to keep up with your material demands. Season tickets to the Dolphins. A second home in Miami. Cars. Clothes. A fucking yacht, for fuck's sake! Neither of us knows how to sail, but your boy toy Chucky does."

"Charles has nothing to do with this."

"Oh, it does when you started seeing him not two years after we married." Beatrix made a scoffing noise, but Doc continued. "You think I didn't know? I did. I just didn't care. The only thing I didn't like was that Caroline knew. I didn't want her to see her father as stupid, so she and I talked about it. I explained that I didn't care if you and I were together. My only priority was her. I did what I had to do by staying with you in order to provide her with as stable a home environment as I could." The more he talked the madder I got at Beatrix. How could this woman, the mother of Doc's child, have no more loyalty to him than this?

"As if she ever did. You were never there."

"That's where you're wrong, Trix. I was there. You thought I was working so you left her with a sitter to go see Chucky. I didn't work nearly as much as you thought. It was me and Linnie's secret."

"I hate you! You're a lousy bastard!"

"Doc!" The door opened, the bell on the handle chiming merrily. "Sorry I'm late. I had to make sure the summons was delivered to -- Oh! Mrs. Collins. I'm so sorry to interrupt." The man was almost as big as Doc. Tall and immaculately dressed, he had an expensive-looking haircut and a neatly trimmed beard, both rich and dark in color. I thought I recognized him from TV somewhere, but I couldn't place him.

"Wrath, this is my ex-wife. Beatrix Collins, soon to be Beatrix Westmore once again. Unless she marries Chucky, though I don't see that happening."

"Yeah, I remember her from your custody battle before the divorce." Wrath said with a grin as he moved around Beatrix and took a seat in the booth across from us. "And I think you're right about Chucky. Especially since the little prick is playing hide the wiener with Gordon Correll's daughter. Thinks he can ride her old man's coattails all the way to the US Senate. I got news for the man; she's got her hands on as many men as he has women. That woman is way out of his league, and he's too stupid to notice." Wrath chuckled as he picked up the papers Trix had scattered all over the table when she threw them at me. "Oh! I see you got the summons. Wonderful! The custody thing shouldn't take but a minute of your time." Wrath pulled out a neatly folded packet of papers fastened to a light blue back from the breast pocket of his immaculate suit and handed it to her. "Normally, I'd deliver this to your lawyer, but since you didn't bring him, you can give it to him. Have your lawyer look it over. The court date is on the first page. This afternoon at five."

"This can't be real," she scoffed, not taking the documents. "The courthouse closes at four-thirty!"

"Well..." Wrath rubbed the back of his neck sheepishly. "I might have pulled a few strings to get this case on the docket. I mean, for the good of your daughter this needs to be settled as quickly as possible."

Beatrix lifted her chin. "Jude knows my terms, and I'm not budging."

Wrath looked confused as he looked back to Doc. "Terms? She talkin' 'bout the five mil she said she'd take to relinquish custody of your daughter?"

Doc shrugged. "That's what the woman said."

Beatrix slammed her palms down on the table, getting right in Doc's face. "And not one cent less, you bastard," she hissed, baring her teeth.

"Not really sure why you're stopping there," Wrath said, leaning back in his seat, picking up a menu and glancing over it as he spoke. "I mean, you owe at least three times that to some pretty unsavory characters. Or, at least, Chucky does."

Beatrix snapped her gaze to Wrath's and straightened slowly. "What do you mean, Charles does?" She asked the question slowly, like she was equal parts disbelieving and also getting a sinking feeling.

"You didn't know?" Wrath looked puzzled, tilting his head like he couldn't believe she was just now learning this. "Honey, why do you think Chucky's been sleeping with a woman ten years his senior and planning to marry a different woman with high political connections? No offense, you're a beautiful woman, but your attitude could suck the ass right out of a good time on the best of days." Beatrix looked like she'd been slapped, her lips parted in a gasp and her eyes wide as saucers. "He owes money. You know he does, because you borrowed money for him."

"It was a one-time thing."

"For you, maybe. But he borrowed more money on your behalf right after you borrowed. Same shark. Now, you're in for three times what you thought you were." Wrath didn't pull any punches. I could almost feel sorry for Beatrix, but that ship had sailed along with the accusations she'd thrown Doc's way.

"Fine." Beatrix shrugged as if it didn't matter, but the sweat that trickled from her hairline down her face told a different story. So did her slight trembling. "Triple it, Jude. Fifteen and you can have it the way you spelled it out."

"Oh, I'll get it the way I spelled it out no matter what." He nodded at Wrath. "That's what he's for."

"At our hearing this evening, I'm going to lay out to the judge what I found. I'm going to present to him the theory that your daughter will be in significant danger since you owe so much money to a known loan shark with a brutal reputation. I'm going to outline the good Salvation's Bane does for the community, how Doc helps children with cancers and doesn't charge them beyond what their insurance pays -- even knowing it could affect his ability to take insurances at all -- and how he makes deals with drug companies with the sole purpose of getting children the treatments they need to survive without breaking the banks of their parents. I'm going to paint Doc here as a pillar of the community one step away from sainthood who only wants his daughter safe. You're going to get dragged through the mud, but more importantly, your business will be a matter of public record. You'll be a liability for your... creditors. What do you think will happen next?"

Wrath had gone from congenial and slightly confused about the situation to a man who not only knew his business but was firmly in control. I had to fight myself to stay focused on my plate and not smirk at Beatrix. I knew I should be sympathetic, but I couldn't find it inside me. Not after the way she'd made it seem like Doc didn't care about Caroline.

Beatrix looked thoroughly cowed. And scared out of her mind. "Jude," she pleaded. Now, she looked around the diner at all the people listening and cringed. She'd started it. Doc had sat there, taking it but knowing what was about to happen and didn't stop any of it. "Please."

Doc stared at her. There was no malice on his face, but no give either. He said nothing, but Wrath opened the folded documents Beatrix hadn't bothered to take when he'd offered them. "We can do all that, *or...*" Wrath took a pen from a front pocket in his suit and handed it to her. "You can sign your rights away now and go back to your maiden name. I have all the proper documents for both as well as the paperwork to change the name on all your accounts. Choice is yours."

"Even if I agree to this, the money --"

"Your loan shark's writing you off as a bad debt." Wrath interrupted with a sneer. "You can thank Doc for that. Let's just say they are more afraid of Doc than they are of losing face. But you may want to leave the city. And you aren't getting any more money from Doc, either. Every single dollar he gave you he recorded. By my calculations he's more than paid child support for Caroline until she turns twenty-three. So, he's done. Not with Caroline, but with you."

"How am I supposed to live? I can't even pay the rent if you don't help me."

Doc shrugged. "My suggestion would be to get a job. You've got a degree. Use it."

"My degree is in Popular Culture! What am I supposed to do with that? At least keep giving me the alimony you were ordered to pay."

"Sorry, Trix. You're signing that away too." He pointed to the papers Wrath had laid out for her. "You can fight it, of course. But any influence Wrath has with your creditors evaporates if this goes to court."

"Just when I think I can't hate you more, you hold my life hostage." Beatrix snatched the pen from Wrath and signed several pages where he indicated. Wrath was now as professional as any lawyer could be. I could see why he was named Wrath from the brief glimpse I'd seen of his ruthless side.

Once done, Wrath handed her a manila envelope. "In there you'll find your new ID, passport, bank and credit cards, and checks, along with all the correct paperwork. You're now Ms. Beatrix Westmore. Everything is legal."

Beatrix snatched the envelope from Wrath and gave Doc a hate-filled look. "I wish I'd never met you."

"I'd say the feeling was mutual, but if I hadn't met you, I wouldn't have Linnie. She's worth any amount of grief."

"Well, now that's settled." Wrath raised a hand to signal Marge he was ready to order. The older woman was all smiles. She passed Beatrix as the other woman left in a huff but didn't acknowledge her. Everyone else went back to eating. If there were a few raised eyebrows and whispers, what did it really matter? Sure, it was uncomfortable, but if it meant Beatrix was out of Doc's life, I couldn't really say it wasn't worth it.

"How's Caroline going to take this?" I had to know. I mean, Beatrix was the girl's mother.

"She'll be OK with it. She told me last week she didn't like Chucky, and Trix accused her of trying to get me and her back together. Which couldn't be further from the truth. Linnie is a smart girl. It hurts for her to think her mother doesn't want her, but she knows. We'll keep an eye on Trix, so I know where she is. If Linnie wants to see her mother, she can. Even if she takes my advice and moves, I'd never deprive Linnie of her mother."

"And even if she doesn't move, she won't be bothered. I've taken care of her creditors as well as her asshole boyfriend." Wrath grinned evilly. Yeah. Wasn't touching that one.

"Don't know why you look at the menu, young man." Marge smiled happily as she set a plate filled with the biggest burger I'd ever seen and fries mounded high all around it. "You always order the same thing every single time."

Wrath looked sheepish before eyeing his burger with hunger. "Thanks, Marge. You're the best."

"Where's your lovely wife? I haven't seen her in too long."

Wrath grinned up at Marge. "She's with the boys today. They've got a baseball game in Miami. I'll be headed that way to meet up with them once my business is concluded. I'll send them all your love."

"Please do. Those boys are wild, and I love them dearly. Holly's good?"

Wrath gave a fierce scowl then. "Girl's gonna be

the death of me, and I may have to kill Fury's kid, Jax."

"Oh? He's in his thirties, isn't he? That's hardly a kid. Besides, what does one have to do with the other?"

"Jax has decided Holly is his." His expression was now thunderous. "Fucker's just askin' for a beatin'." The second his anger took over, Wrath's language deteriorated like every other biker I'd been around. I couldn't help but smile. I covered my amusement by burying my face against Doc's arm.

"OK," Marge frowned. "How does that mean Holly's going to be the death of you?"

"Because, even though she fusses at him and berates him, I also see the looks she gives him. I'm not pleased."

Marge and Doc both burst out laughing. Doc outright guffawed until tears were rolling down his face. "I'm sorry, Wrath. Honest. But that's the funniest shit. You're gonna have Fury's son for a son-in-law. Noelle will eat you alive."

"Shut the fuck up, asshole. Wait until Caroline takes up with some jackass. See how funny it is then."

"Never happening. She's not dating until she's at least forty. Besides, I'm a doctor. I know how to kill a man so no one realizes he's been murdered, and I make sure everyone knows it."

"Yeah? Let me know how that works out for ya when you tell your little princess you accidentally might have murdered her boyfriend on purpose." Wrath gave Doc the finger.

The food was marvelous, as always. The men kept bantering back and forth, laughing like nothing was amiss. Like they hadn't just changed Beatrix's life forever.

"Much as I hate to leave good company," Wrath said, wiping his mouth, "I've got to get back to the office. I've filed everything in anticipation of your ex-wife's compliance, but I wasn't lying when I told her I'd scheduled the hearing this evening. I need to let Judge Wilson know we worked everything out. Then I'm off to Miami."

Wrath stood and Doc stood with him, sticking out his hand. "Your help is greatly appreciated, brother. Give Holly and Celeste my love."

"I will. Call on me anytime. It's cooperation like this that will strengthen both our clubs."

Doc sat back beside me again, leaning in to give me a soft kiss. "You ready to go?"

"Can we take the long way back to the compound? I might be addicted to riding behind you."

Doc chuckled softly and kissed me again. "We can ride anywhere you want to, baby. Just tell me where you want to go."

"Just back to the clubhouse. I'm sure you'll need to talk with Caroline and let her know what's going on. I still hate that she's essentially cut off from her mother, even if the woman is a serious bitch."

"Linnie will be fine. Like I said, I'd never keep her from her mother. Not if she wanted to see Trix. She's old enough to make up her own mind about those kinds of things. If she wants to see or talk to Trix, it will happen. I'll move heaven and earth to make it happen."

"And this is one of many reasons I love you. And yes, I caught what you said earlier. Did you mean it?" If I sounded a little vulnerable, I gave myself permission. "I get that you needed to show Beatrix you'd moved on, and I'm OK with that. I just want to know --"

Doc pulled me closer for a gentle but persistent kiss. "Relax, baby. I wouldn't have said I love you if it weren't true. How it happened so fast, I have no idea, but I'm not fighting it. We're going to make this work, and we're gonna have one hell of a good time doing it."

I smiled, and Doc kissed me again. "Come on. Let's get outta here and back home. We'll talk to Caroline, and all of us will outline what we expect from each other."

"I think that's a great idea."

Doc put some bills on the table to take care of the tab and a tip. Then he threw up his hand at Tito and Marge before we left the diner to get on his bike and take off. I was smiling ear to ear. The sun warmed my face. The breeze whipped through my hair. With sheer joy, I turned my face up to the sky and whooped. Doc chuckled at my antics but didn't seem to mind. He did as I'd asked and took the long way home. I'd never felt so free in my life. I was in love with a wonderful man who loved me back. His daughter was good with it, and I'd already loved her before I met Doc. Life was good. I had a feeling it would only get better from here.

Chapter Eight

Doc

The next few weeks were uneventful. Thorn and Havoc were in closed-door meetings with Rocket and his vice president, Claw. They were in Thorn's office twenty hours a day. Sometimes, I saw Thorn and Havoc leaving the room with deep frowns as they marched through the compound to Thorn's suite. Last week, both men looked pale when they exited, like they'd seen a ghost or something, but still looked as hard as I'd ever seen either of them.

"Odd," I muttered as I glanced back at the two men when we passed in the hall. Neither spoke or made eye contact. Both looked equal parts determined and resigned.

"What is?" Lia looked up at me, a questioning look on her face. She seemed truly happy. She and Linnie got on well. Since moving into my house, she'd made herself at home. One thing I never thought I'd be making room for was a baby grand piano. I'd had the boys start on a studio for Lia and an extra bathroom addition. No way could a house have two women living in it and only one bathroom.

"Thorn. He's been in meetings with your father and Claw. Every time they come out of his office, both he and Havoc look worse for wear. That's saying something, because they're both hardasses."

"I hope everything's OK." Now Lia looked distressed when she hadn't before.

"I'm sure everything's all right. No one has asked to talk to you or me, so anything going on involves the two clubs in some way or another. I'll tell you if there's any need to worry."

She nodded, but I could see she was still

concerned. "All right. Just make sure you do. I don't want to cause problems for a club that has been so wonderful to me. Nor to you." She wrapped her arms around my waist as we walked. "You've been so wonderful, Doc. Thank you for playing along with my father when he gave me to you." She giggled as she spoke. "That's so wrong. Who gives their daughter away?"

"He didn't give you away." I chuckled. "I took you. And I ain't givin' you back." I scooped her up over my shoulder and hurried outside. Lia squealed, grabbing hold of the waist of my pants as she held on.

"Put me down, you ape!" She wasn't mad. There was laughter in her voice, but she continued to make her little demands. I grinned and swatted her ass.

When we got to the pool, I put her on her feet before tugging off her shirt and shorts to reveal the deep red bikini underneath. Once I had her clothes off, I tossed her in the pool. She gave a shriek before splashdown. By the time she'd surfaced, I'd stripped off my cut, folding it in half and draping it over the back of a chair. I tossed my shirt in the general direction of my cut, and I toed off my shoes. My jeans followed, leaving me bare-ass naked. Lia gave a whoop of disbelief, then I dove into the pool after her.

She'd turned and kicked away, racing to the other side of the large pool, but I caught her, snagging her ankle and pulling her to me as I took us both to the surface. Lia's laughter warmed my soul, and I was grateful I could do that for her. She'd been so somber and nearly withdrawn when I first met her, but now she was blossoming. I only prayed I'd had at least a small part in her transformation.

Lia laughed, her face tilted up to let the sun kiss her face. Which made me jealous. So I kissed her myself. With a sigh, Lia wrapped her arms around my neck and kissed me back. It didn't take long for the encounter to become heated.

One of the many things I adored about Lia was her willingness to follow where I led. Since I'd taken her virginity, she'd jumped in with both feet. She'd even initiated sex a few times in the last week or so. I loved her enthusiasm. And, honestly, the girl was becoming a seriously good lover. She paid attention to my responses to her. Even though I tried to make sex all about her and her pleasure, Lia took it as a personal challenge to drive me out of my fucking mind.

She wrapped her legs around my waist as she continued to kiss me. I knew she didn't like exposing herself in public, even if there was no one around, so I left her bikini on. Didn't mean I was above groping a tit. Small as they were, the nipples were luscious and pouty when she was aroused. I love seeing and feeling them jut against her top. She cried out and arched her back, pushing her breasts against my palm.

Before she could protest, I pulled one triangle aside and latched on to her nipple. I pulled hard before nipping gently. Then I swirled my tongue around it to ease any lingering ache. That seemed to hit her pretty hard, because she screamed and her legs tightened around my waist as she ground her pussy against my cock.

"Fuck!" she cried out, shuddering in my arms. "Do that again!"

With a growl, I did. I pulled the triangle back into place before tugging the other one aside and giving that nipple the same treatment. All the while, Lia slid up and down my length through her bikini bottoms. I pulled back to kiss her again, barely remembering to cover her breast.

Our kisses became more and more frantic. My breathing grew deep, my heart pounding. I practically shook with the need to fuck her.

"This is what you've reduced me to, woman," I growled against her lips. "I'm about to come against you. Ain't done that since I was a fuckin' teenager!"

"Doc! Fuck!" Her cries sounded as frantic as my grunts and growls, which were near constant as I tried my damnedest to stave off coming.

"I've gotcha, baby. Can you come for me?"

"NO!" She snapped her gaze to me, her eyes wide when they'd been closed in bliss. "Not coming until you're inside me!" Without waiting for me to decide what I needed to do, Lia reached between us and tugged her bikini bottoms aside. The elastic rubbed against my dick as she pushed my cock into the velvety soft cunt.

Fuck... Me...

"What the fuck'er you doin', Lia?" I was desperate to hold my cum. We hadn't talked about it, and I wasn't sure she was ready even if it was a fantasy coming true for me. "I'm gonna fuckin' come if you don't get me out of that fuckin' sweet pussy." My body jerked, needing to fuck her like I needed to breathe.

"Ain't lettin' you out of me," she whimpered. "Ain't doin' it!" She locked her legs even tighter around me before she started to ride me like she was riding a bucking bronco. She cried out and grunted as she exerted herself, water sloshing and splashing in a violent white-water cap.

The next thing I knew, she was screaming at the top of her lungs, and her cunt gripped me like a fuckin' vise. I actually thought she might strangle my dick, the spasm was so hard. And she didn't stop moving! With each contraction of her pussy around my cock, with each violent rise and fall of her body, I grew closer and closer to the point of no return.

Then she mashed her lower body against mine as hard as she could, falling back so she nearly went under the water. I caught her, barely, but it took my concentration away from not coming. So I did. And sweet God almighty, I thought I was going to fucking die!

There was no holding back my orgasm. It was happening and, try as I might, I couldn't push her off me. One, she was latched on tight as a tick, not letting go willingly without me hurting her. That was my excuse. The second reason was because I didn't try that fuckin' hard to get her off. I was right where I wanted to be and, since she'd started it, I was only too happy to take what she was offering.

When I came, I couldn't even bellow my satisfaction. The air seized in my lungs, my muscles spasmed. The pressure built and built until finally, *finally*, my cum exploded from me with such force I was afraid I might have pulled something. Even in the water, my knees gave out, and I sank beneath the water. I tried to shove Lia off me again, but she wrapped her arms around me tighter and kissed me for all she was worth, breathing for me. I sucked her in greedily before pushing us to the surface. Even then I reached out blindly for the side of the pool, moving so Lia could reach the tiled ledge.

I felt like I'd run a marathon. My lungs burned, and the sweetest lethargy washed over me. All I could do was lean on the edge of the pool and hold Lia against me to protect her as much as I could. Lord knew, I was past doing much, but I was going to try, dammit!

"Wow." Lia giggled slightly even as she clung to

me, breathing as hard as I was. "That was…"

"Yeah, no shit." My own chuckle sounded more than a little strained. "I think you killed me."

"If I killed you, you killed me. I'm not sure I can move."

"Don't need to, baby. Just lean against me. I'll keep us afloat." I snorted. "Somehow."

That brought more giggles from Lia, followed by a deep, contented sigh. "Thank you, Doc. I suppose I should have talked to you about this first, but thank you for giving it to me."

I pulled her back in for another gentle kiss. The thought of what we'd done got me hard. Didn't take long for me to realize I wanted her again. Reaching between us, I held her gaze as I guided my cock back inside her sweet pussy. Her eyes widened slightly before going hooded with contentment.

"Make no mistake, baby. I did exactly what I wanted to do. I was trying to protect you, but you had to go and demand my cum."

"Would it help if I demanded it again?" She was a siren, luring me to my doom. If that were the case, I was going willingly.

I moved inside her, taking my time and savoring the hot sweetness. She was tight. I could feel her heart beating frantically all around my dick. She was more passive now, letting me take control. I had no idea what the fuck I would do if she grew impatient with me again. She'd take what she wanted, and I'd shout to the heavens.

"You sure you're OK with this?" I kissed her cheek and nipped her earlobe. Lia shivered and tightened her thighs around me, like she was afraid I was going to try to back out again. As if!

"I am, Doc. I want all of you, and I want you to

have all of me."

"We shouldn't do this on a whim, but I'm not takin' it back. Now that I've come in you once, you'll have to tell me to pull out."

"Never." She sighed and kissed me again. I slid her up and down my length. The water churned around us, though at a much more manageable rate. I took Lia with all the love I had for her inside me. And I did love her. I'd known it when I'd told Beatrix as much, but I hadn't truly felt it this powerfully. Lia was mine. Forever. I'd do anything I had to keep her. "I love you, Doc. Love you so freaking much!"

That was all I could take. I strained, trying to hold back until I could take Lia with me. I slipped my thumb between us and found her clit. The second I pressed, rubbing in tight circles, she came apart, screaming once again. My cock exploded inside her, bathing her inside with hot, sticky cum. I was a bastard for hoping it took hold and got her pregnant, but it was the foremost thought in my mind. I wanted her pregnant with my kid. I wanted everyone in the whole fuckin' world to know she was mine.

"Christ, I love you, Lia! So fuckin' much!"

I shuddered as I came down once again. I held Lia tightly to me, stroking her back as she came down with me. I wanted to take her to bed and make love to her the rest of the night, but I wasn't even sure I could get us out of the pool safely at the moment.

We were laughing lightly with each other when a commotion rose from inside the compound. The door exploded open, and Thorn stormed out with Havoc hot on his heels. Mariana, Thorn's woman, was protesting loudly from her position over Thorn's shoulder.

"Put me down, Thorn. Stop acting like a caveman!"

"What the fuck, Ana? Why are you so calm about this!" Thorn set Ana on her feet but pulled her away from the door to the clubhouse and put her between himself and Havoc. The VP had his phone out, texting furiously.

"Good Goddamned thing the other girls went out this evening. Told Styx and Justice to keep them away from here until I give the OK." Havoc spoke softly, but looked as freaked out as Thorn was.

"What's going on?" Lia called out her question. I'd have preferred her not to draw their attention for several reasons, but most of all because I wanted the element of surprise if I needed to attack to defend my brothers. But also I wasn't certain her bathing suit was entirely put to rights, and I had no wish for the other men to get an eyeful.

"Hush, baby," I said, though I thought the damage was done. Surprisingly, none of them seemed to notice us. I pressed my lips to her temple and sank us deeper into the water so I could barely see above the side.

"There's no reason to get so bent out of shape, Thorn." Mariana tried to soothe her husband, but Thorn didn't seem to be capable of letting her. "If they'd wanted to hurt us, they would have already. He only told you everything because he needed you to understand why he needs your help. All things considered, you should be flattered he thinks Salvation's Bane and Black Reign are capable of this. Didn't sound to me like just anyone could do it, but he's convinced all of you can."

I wasn't sure who "he" was, but instinctively knew I didn't want to know.

"Ana --"

"No, Thorn! Listen to me. No one has to know

everything. El Diablo, Samson, and possibly El Segador, but not everyone."

"I can't keep something like this from the club!"

"We may have to, brother." Havoc scrubbed a hand over his face. "At least for the time being. If they need to know, we can always fill them in later. Besides, Ana knows. You know I'll have to tell Spring. Not sure it'll make much difference. The Black Reign men will tell their women same as we do. That's too many people trying to keep secrets. It'll slip."

"This is a good way for someone to get killed." Thorn wasn't happy, but I could see he was going to take Havoc's suggestion into consideration. "We've got a week or so. I'll call El Diablo and set up a meeting. Will probably need to get Cain involved, but only if we have to."

"Fuck." Havoc laced his hands behind his neck. "We're so fucking fucked."

"I don't think we are," Ana said gently, her arm gripping Thorn's shoulder. "It will all be good. I want you to make sure everyone knows to be extra careful. I don't want anyone getting hurt because they weren't prepared."

"You always want to see the good in people, Mariana," Thorn said, but I could tell he was relaxing by degrees. "Given your past and how you were betrayed, if you can do it, I'll manage it too. Different doesn't mean bad. It means we need to find a common ground and treat them like we would any other club."

This sounded serious. I looked at Lia, and she was frowning in their direction. Not like she was mad, just puzzled. "What's going on?" she whispered.

"Not sure, honey."

"We should let them know we're here. They'll think we're eavesdropping."

"Not yet." I had a feeling this was something I needed to know, but honestly, what difference was it going to make? If this was about Grim Road -- and I was sure it was -- it didn't change the fact I was keeping Lia. The only thing that might be useful would be to know in advance anything that might affect Lia or her family so I could prepare her gently.

"OK. It's settled, then. We'll brief the people Rocket named, then see how it plays out. Above all, we have to make sure Doc keeps Talia safe. Rocket insisted on this."

"We both know that was more for everyday living than any situation he's got going on. Doc claimed Talia properly. The wedding ceremony still has to happen, but the license has been signed and filed. Doc insisted on it. Not only that, Talia got a tattoo proclaiming her property of Doc. No one'll be able to contest his claim. Rocket said so himself." Havoc seemed to shrug Thorn's warning off. Which was a good fucking thing, because the thought that my brothers weren't sure if I could protect my woman made me want to bust a motherfucker up.

"Good. We're of the same opinion. I just needed to hear you say it. What about Caroline? You believe him when he says she was perfectly safe?"

"I shouldn't, but I think I do. If there was a possibility of anything happening to her, he'd have told us directly when he was asked. Instead, he'd looked like I'd insulted him and his entire club."

"I know this is difficult to accept, Thorn, but I think everything will work out. It's all going to be good."

"I hope you're right."

"I am. You'll see." Mariana smiled up at Thorn and hooked her arm around his as the three of them went back inside.

"Wow," Lia said when the door had closed, and we exited the pool to retrieve our clothing. "That wasn't intense or cryptic or anything."

"Not at all."

"You going to talk to him about it?" I looked down into her face. There was nothing there but curiosity. She wasn't afraid or resigned. Which meant she was in the dark, same as me.

"No," I said, knowing it was the truth. "If Thorn thinks we need to know, he'll tell us. Until then, we'll both be extra vigilant until your dad gets back from whatever job he's taken away from here. If something changes, we'll reevaluate." I brushed a kiss over her mouth. "Make no mistake, though, Lia, we'll decide together. We're a team. You scared?" If she was, I'd go to Thorn tonight and demand to know. In any other environment, I'd have done it. At the hospital. My clinic. Literally any other situation. But this was my club. My brothers. Thorn was our president. I'd trust him to know when he needed to tell me.

She smiled up at me. "No. I trust you. If you trust your club, I will too. I follow you."

"And we work together."

"Together."

Epilogue

The bombshell my father dropped in the lap of Salvation's Bane was unbelievable at best. Until he proved what he was saying was true. I now understood why Thorn and Havoc had been shaken that night by the pool. What I didn't understand was how Mariana accepted it so readily. I was barely able to wrap my mind around it, and I'd lived in the middle of them. No matter. I believed my dad and Claw when they told me I was safe and that Caroline was never in any danger. Grim Road was many things, but they didn't harm innocents. No one was more innocent than Caroline.

Even with everything that had happened, I was surprised I wasn't panicking or questioning everything I'd ever known about myself and my family. Somehow, I took it in stride. Probably shock. I was sure I'd lose my mind later.

Right now, Doc held me on his lap as we looked out at the ocean. It was almost sunrise, and he'd brought me out here away from everyone to talk. We'd talked for the better part of an hour, sitting in a wooden beach chair with me curled up in his lap. The breeze was pleasantly cool on my skin, and the sound of the waves crashing over the beach was a soothing music to the current scene.

"You OK? He dropped a lot on you."

"Yeah. I'm good. I was surprised to find out he wasn't really my dad, though. I never suspected. He always treated me like a daughter."

"He gave his word to his brother in arms to look out for you. I'd say he fulfilled that promise. I also happen to believe he loves you very much. You might not be his daughter by blood, but you are the daughter of his heart."

"While I'm glad to know there won't be any complications in your life, I kind of wish I was like him. You know. That I could do the things he does."

"Honey, it wouldn't matter to me if you were. You're mine, and I'll never let you go, no matter what craziness your family brings." He chuckled. "That would be something, though."

I giggled. "Yeah. It would be."

"Turn around. Straddle me."

I did, putting my knees on either side of his hips and draping myself on top of him. Doc threaded his hands through my hair and angled my head exactly the way he wanted it so he could kiss me thoroughly. I sighed into the kiss and let him have me. Since we'd started having sex, Doc had never let me leave his arms unsatisfied. I was happy to let him teach me what he liked. Hell, he taught me what *I* liked. Every time was an adventure to me. I loved the way he loved me.

The beach we lazed on was the club's private beach. I was told they frequently had amphibious drills or something. Most of the men here, including Doc, worked for a paramilitary organization they called ExFil. At this moment, I didn't care why they had a private beach, only that it was private.

I sat up, bracing my hands on Doc's naked chest. He'd shucked his shirt when we'd first gotten there, and I'd lain against him, better able to take in his masculine scent. I leaned in to flick my tongue over one nipple while I unbuttoned my own shirt. It fluttered to the sand while I pulled the string on my bikini top and tossed it to lie with my shirt.

Doc grunted, his hands going to my chest

automatically. He squeezed and kneaded my tits and twisted my nipples gently. "You're so fuckin' beautiful, Lia. I hope you know that."

"You're beautiful too," I said with a smile. "There's nothing about you I don't sincerely love."

"I love you too, baby. Now. You wantin' my cock?"

I grinned. "You know me so well already."

"When it comes to sex, yes. I'm still learning about you. Which, by the way, the boys finished the addition to the house. I have a surprise for you when we get home. Only you have to promise to use it immediately. I want to see if it was worth it or not." The look on his face said he knew it was totally worth it, but he wanted to see if I'd take the challenge. He should have known.

"Challenge accepted. What am I doing?"

"Right now? You're unzippin' my pants, pulling off your bikini bottoms, and takin' me into that sweet, hot pussy."

Yeah. There was no way I was denying him that. I was pretty sure we made enough noise to bring any bystanders, but no one disturbed us. When we both lay there, spent, I laughed for the sheer joy of it all. I was on a beautiful stretch of beach with a man I adored, making love in the sand. What was there not to be joyful about?

Once we got home, Caroline welcomed us inside the house. One of the newer patched members -- I think his name was Lock -- was with Caroline, watching her while me and her dad were away. He was the one to open the door, though it was obvious Caroline had forced the issue. She looked at him with annoyance before she threw herself into my arms with a huge smile.

"You're staying, aren't you, Talia?"

"Wild horses couldn't drag me away."

"Or wolves. Or bears, even," Doc muttered under his breath.

I shot him a look of annoyance. He tried to hide his grin, but I saw it. I stuck my tongue out at him.

"Got something you can do with that tongue later," he whispered wickedly in my ear.

"Come on, Talia!" Caroline was practically bouncing with excitement.

"What's all this?" I laughed as she tugged my hand until I had to quicken my pace to follow her to the newly finished addition Doc had had built onto the house. When she opened the double French doors to the room, I gasped, my mouth hanging open.

The room was hardwood with a large area rug in one inside corner away from the windows. The walls were a muted blue, with the plush furniture a deeper blue. On the rug, a white baby grand piano rested, the lid up and begging to be played.

Tears formed in my eyes, and my hands flew to my mouth as a soft sob escaped. "When did you do this?"

"While you and Dad were gone," Caroline said cheerfully. "We wanted it to be a surprise."

"Well," I sniffed as I laughed tearfully. "It certainly is a surprise!"

"Well?" Doc brushed a kiss in my hair. "I told you I expected you to use it. Play us something."

I nodded eagerly and walked to the piano, a little in awe of the beautiful instrument. "I don't know what to say. It's so beautiful."

"Consider it my wedding gift to you, Lia. And it's not half as beautiful as you."

"Awwww," Caroline gushed. "That's so sweet,

Dad! I didn't know you were a romantic!"

"I ain't. And if you tell anyone, I'll swear you lied."

Caroline giggled and wrapped her arms around her father's waist as she watched me. I could tell she was anxious for me to play. She was probably anxious to play it herself.

There were so many songs I wanted to play for these two special people in my life. So much music that spoke to me so clearly, but I wanted to convey my love in one song. A song of hope and family. Of unconditional love.

I chose a song by Billy Joel. "Lullabye (Goodnight My Angel)."

As I let the chords of the simple but beautiful song flow from my fingers, I was struck at all I'd gained. A daughter. A husband who loved me. A huge extended family who had proven they'd protect me. Friends I knew I'd love for the rest of my life. Most of all, I found myself. And that part of me would always be in Doc's arms. Jude Collins. I was now Talia Collins. We'd have a ceremony soon, but I would never be more content than I was as I glanced up at the two people who meant more to me than anything else in the world. They watched me with rapt attention, soft smiles on their faces.

And the music continued. Surrounding us. Filling our home with... *Love*.

Marteeka Karland

Marteeka Karland is an international bestselling author who leads a double life as an erotic romance author by evening and a semi-domesticated housewife by day. Known for her down and dirty MC romances, Marteeka takes pleasure in spinning tales of tenacious, protective heroes and spirited, vulnerable heroines. She staunchly advocates that every character deserves a blissful ending, even, sometimes, the villains in her narratives. Her writings are speckled with intense, raw elements resulting in page-turning delight entwined with seductive escapades leading up to gratifying conclusions that elicit a sigh from her readers.

Away from the keyboard, Marteeka finds joy in baking and supporting her husband with their gardening activities. The late summer season is set aside for preserving the delightful harvest that springs from their combined efforts (which is mostly his efforts, but you can count it). To stay updated with Marteeka's latest adventures and forthcoming books, make sure to visit her website. Don't forget to register for her newsletter which will pepper you with a potpourri of Teeka's beloved recipes, book suggestions, autograph events, and a plethora of interesting tidbits.

Marteeka at Changeling: changelingpress.com/ marteeka-karland-a-39

Changeling Press E-Books

More Sci-Fi, Fantasy, Paranormal, and BDSM adventures available in e-book format for immediate download at ChangelingPress.com -- Werewolves, Vampires, Dragons, Shapeshifters and more -- Erotic Tales from the edge of your imagination.

What are E-Books?

E-books, or electronic books, are books designed to be read in digital format -- on your desktop or laptop computer, notebook, tablet, Smart Phone, or any electronic e-book reader.

Where can I get Changeling Press E-Books?

Changeling Press e-books are available at ChangelingPress.com, Amazon, Apple Books, Barnes & Noble, and Kobo/Walmart.

Changeling Press, LLC

ChangelingPress.com